Everyday

Lee Rourke

social disease

First published 2007 by Social Disease, UK.
11 Haymans Point, Tyers Street, London.

www.socialdisease.co.uk

Book design by Paul Cox

ISBN 0-9552829-4-2

About the Author

Lee Rourke is a Mancunian who resides in Hackney, East London. He is the founder and editor of Scarecrow and a co-editor at 3AM Magazine. His writing, both fiction and non-fiction, regularly appears in The Guardian, The Observer, Dazed and Confused Magazine, BLATT, Lamport Court, 3AM Magazine, Zygote in My Coffee, Straight From The Fridge, RSB, Laura Hird's writing showcase, Writing at the Edge (edited by Zsolt Alapi) and many others. Blaise Cendrars is his saviour.

Acknowledgements

Heartfelt gratitude to Matthew Coleman for his tenacity, A. Stevens for his realism and Andrew Gallix for his insight and meticulous editorial skills. Honourable mentions to Tom McCarthy, Stewart Home, Tony O'Neill, Ben Myers, Paul Ewen and Adelle Stripe.

Earlier versions of some of the fragments contained in this anthology have appeared in the following online and print publications: Writing at the Edge (edited by Zsolt Alapi, Sirensong Books, 2007), 3AM Magazine, BLATT, laurahird.com, Zygote in my Coffee, Paris Bitter Hearts Pit, The Beat, and Lamport Court.

Heidi James I am indebted to you.

For Holly

Table of Contents

Our narratives seem unfair – they are frequently broken and discontinuous, they have no ending.

Jock Young, 'The Vertigo of Late Modernity'

But I do not think even Sisyphus is required to scratch himself, or to groan, or to rejoice, as the fashion is now, always at the same appointed places. And it may even be they are not too particular about the route he takes provided it gets him to his destination safely and on time. And perhaps he thinks each journey is his first. This would keep hope alive, would it not, hellish hope. Whereas to see yourself doing the same thing endlessly over and over again fills you with satisfaction.

Samuel Beckett, 'Molloy, Part II'

Introduction

Unlike his characters[1], Lee Rourke doesn't go unnoticed. The first time we met was in the toilet at Filthy MacNasty's where he'd cornered me during a gig organised by *3:AM Magazine* back in April 2005. Oblivious to the funny looks people were giving us, he waxed lyrical about the literary insurrection we had kick-started five years earlier and were celebrating that night. Somewhere in the background, Shane MacGowan was emptying his bladder to the strains of the Monochrome Set. It was there — in what Joe Orton called the last stronghold of male privilege — that I realised a new scene (the Offbeats) had emerged. And Lee was slap-bang in the middle of it. I already knew of him as the editor of *Scarecrow* who banged the drum for "the unheard, the unconventional, the eccentric, the revolutionary and the radical". I was soon to discover his short stories — as you are now. Brace yourselves.

What can you expect? Well, it all depends whether you squint or not, of course. If you do: 1) David Brent dry-humping Franz Kafka over the zerox machine, 2) an episode of *Nathan Barley* penned by Herman Melville and shot by Mike Leigh, 3) The Rakes fronted by Julian Maclaren-Ross with Patrick Hamilton on bass, Ann Quin on drums and Maurice Blanchot on kazoo. If you don't: pigeons, pints of bitterness, work, Islington, gratuitous violence, boredom, Hackney twits, psychogeography, pigeons, Hoxton twats, anonymous crushes on public transport, class war, urban alienation, media whores, pigeons, happy slapping, sexual frustration, City yuppies, the threat of terrorism, immigrants from Eastern Europe, boredom, work, binge drinking, pigeons, pigeons and more pigeons.

Lee Rourke certainly has his finger on London's tachycardiac pulse, but it is the universal he zeroes in on with obvious relish. In one story, William Blake's sober gravestone suddenly rears into view ("Gravestones"). Baudelaire's captured albatross — a symbol of the impotence of the artist — reappears here in the shape of one of those big advertising placards modern slaves hold up for a living on busy street corners ("The Only Living Boy on Oxford Street"). The tale of the swan that is killed for kicks by a couple of mindless thugs has all the gravitas and pathos of a Greekish deicide. The pole dancer whose rotting flesh decomposes with every new gyration echoes Webster's skull beneath the skin ("Night Shift").

Alongside the ubiquitous pigeons, the emblem of this collection is surely the photocopying machine. This is why the figure of Sisyphus looms so large, from the hypnotic sway of a woman's rump in "Cruel Work" to the *Groundhog Day* pattern[2] of "Footfalls". After being knocked over by a runaway bus, a man is condemned to circle round Soho looking in vain for the young woman who had come to his rescue ("Searching For Amy"). Taking his cue from Dante via Eliot, Rourke describes the vicious Circle Line as a noughties version of the nine circles of Hell all rolled into one. The office drones (a keyword) who inhabit these stories are the direct descendants of the living dead crossing London Bridge in *The Waste Land* (minus Eliot's class snobbery). In the author's words, *Everyday* expresses "the realisation that we are fragmenting, falling, and that it is never ending: just repeating".[3] Rourke is fascinated by the straw that breaks the camel's back — the moment when his Bartlebys start running amok or falling apart. As in Michael Andrews' famous painting, people keep falling over, giving in to gravity, endlessly re-enacting their postlapsarian condition[4]. After dropping like flies, they squirm on their backs, Kafkaesque insects, while indifferent passers-by pass them by. Again and again and again. And when they finally get up, they jump back on the conveyor belt. “I’m not what you could describe ‘as going places’,” says the eponymous narrator of “John Barleycorn” reflecting on the treadmill of his life. These characterless characters are always on the go, but theirs is the restlessness of the undead. They are going nowhere fast.

Some of the stories collected here hardly qualify as stories at all. They are vignettes, or “fragments” to use Rourke’s preferred term — fragments of a bigger picture that doesn’t end. There is no complete whole in *Everyday*, just a gaping hole in a pair of black tights, a book of blank pages and an all-pervasive Heideggerian boredom. A gaping whole, but no grand narrative. Lee Rourke “documents the little alleyways and back streets,” which brings us back to the toilet at Filthy MacNasty’s where it all began.

Begin!

Andrew Gallix

Editor-in-Chief, *3:AM Magazine*

Université de Paris IV-Sorbonne, October 2007.

Footnotes:

1) Rourke is fond of aptronyms (Sheila Hole, Elaine Lowbottom or the bibulous John Barleycorn), some of which advertise the characters very banality: "Hack" or "Tony", for instance, are ideal names for everyday Everymen. And then, of course, there's "Anon".

2) Or should that be Wernham Hogg?

3) "Purposely Resisting All That: An Interview With Lee Rourke" by Susan Tomaselli, *Dogmatika*, October 2007.

4) Here, we are very close to the failed transcendence that lies at the heart of Tom McCarthy's work (which Rourke has described as "blueprints" for his own).

The Geography of a Psychopath

The article that I had been reading that day on psychogeography was quite uncomplicated really; it suggested I should:

"Unfold a streetmap of London, place a glass, rim down, anywhere on the map, and draw round its edge. Pick up the map, go out into the city, and walk the circle, keeping as close as you can to the curve. Record the experiences as you go, in whatever medium you favour: film, photography, manuscript, tape." (A road of one's own, Robert MacFarlane).

So I did; and my preferred medium was the mighty Biro, black of course, lightly chewed – I didn't own a camera. I never have. I quickly found an unkempt London A to Z (2005, Ed.) on the shelf by the phone and took a coffee mug from the cluttered kitchen sink. I opened my map on central London and then placed the coffee mug on it. I could see the page absorbing the moisture from the rim; I circled it with the Biro, quite indiscriminately. I lifted the coffee mug once I had finished and marvelled at my perfectly formed circle, pausing momentarily for a closer inspection. It was one of those uncanny moments that happen in your life from time to time – as if kismet had reared its ugly head, out of sheer boredom if anything. The thin, black, perfectly spherical line went directly through my road in Hackney. I could start my own Psychogeograpic walk on my very own doorstep.

[...]

My name is Matt Hamilton and I have recently been made redundant. I have lived in the same house all my life. I inherited it after my parents died; my mother surrendered to cancer (she was a dinner lady at a local comprehensive) and my father was destroyed by alcohol abuse (he was a security guard at a large department store on Oxford Street). I have no siblings. I am fifty-two years of age but most people think I am a lot younger due to my athletic frame and a good thatch of thick jet-black hair. I keep fit because I walk everywhere. I've never owned a car, nor have I wanted to. I find TV alien and the cinema bores me. I want to be a writer but I don't write that much, not because I can't, but because I don't know what to write about. Everything just seems the same to me. Life, put simply, is boring. So, you see, I have a lot of time on my hands. When you've worked most of your life, after leaving school at fifteen with no formal qualifications, it's quite funny the things you'll do to fill up the empty void. Am I happy about losing my job as an Insurance worker? Who knows? Do I want another job? No thank-you. How is getting another job going to improve my life? So, after reading the odd biography here and there, a spot of cooking, cleaning and sleeping I often have enough time to do whatever I want – so I choose to walk. That's my life. It's funny, sitting here, thinking about it and writing it down. Waiting, not knowing what's going to become of me. Not understanding how all this actually happened. You see, it's funny how your life can just change. Nothing is in your own hands. You amount to nothing in the end. None of us do.

[...]

I looked outside my window. It was a gloomy, inclement morning, fast approaching mid-day. I put on my shoes and my long coat; grabbed my new map and stepped outside. The cool, damp air clung to my face like a wet flannel. The door closed behind me. I was outside. It was time to start my walk. I was happy. I'd just one decision to make: whether I should turn left or right when I stepped onto the pavement. I instinctively chose right. Ivy Street was unusually empty except for the red haired woman lying on the pavement in front of me. She immediately blocked my path and I didn't know whether to casually step over her and continue on my way. I was in two minds. I thought about it for a couple of seconds and then decided to crouch down beside her to see what the problem was. An A4 notepad was by her side. I picked it up. I nudged her arm.

"Hullo, are you all right? Have you fallen? Can you hear me?"

"Yes, I can hear you . . ."

"What's the matter with you? Is anything broken? . . ."

"I fell over, would you mind helping me to my feet? How many people are staring over?"

"The street is deserted. Are you okay?"

"Just a little dazed . . ."

I helped her to her feet; she was as tall as me. She had long dark red hair that fell below her shoulders in no particular fashion, but it shined and looked glorious and healthy. It had obviously been dyed that colour. Her skin was pale with slight freckles scattered across her face like little petals. An odd intensity burned behind her eyes, it was hard to judge the colour, but they were most probably blue. Blue eyes are known to be the sexiest – so they say. Or is that green? She was considerably younger than me, maybe in her early thirties – although she could have been younger. Her accent wasn't English, although she spoke it very well, it was most probably Russian – although I could've been wrong about that too. She smiled and looked at me; she didn't seem all that embarrassed to be honest; in fact she seemed quite happy to see me, like a strange familiarity had descended upon us. I handed her back the A4 notepad and she continued to smile.

"Are you thirsty?"

"I was just out for a walk actually . . ."

"Funny, I was just returning from one . . . Would you like to walk with me to my flat? It's just around the corner. I'll fetch you a drink. Coffee? Tea? Whiskey?"

"Whiskey you say?"

"Yes, whiskey . . . Good stuff too . . ."

You could say it was like all my dreams had come true at once. She was quite beautiful, in a rather idiosyncratic way, and I had been lonely for a long time. We walked without saying that much. We dodged discarded kebab wrappers along Pitfield Street and random footballers across Shoreditch Park as we headed north. Her gait was purposeful and she looked at me intensely from time to time – she was dressed in tight jeans, boots and a red woollen jumper; she looked like a librarian, maybe on some university campus or other, but the sort who had a life outside of academia. At first I didn't notice but it soon became apparent that we were following the curve of the black Biro on my map exactly. It seemed like the most natural thing in the world. We eventually arrived at her small flat on Penn Street. A couple of teenagers in hoods were loitering on the corner. The air hung heavy around us as a police helicopter hovered above. I watched her wonderful arse wobble slightly as we entered her block and strode together up the cold stairwell. Once inside I immediately noticed the distinct aroma of earl grey tea. The flat was neat and tidy and crammed with books of every description. We sat close together on her blue sofa without saying a word. Suddenly she leant across and began to kiss me hard, her warm luscious tongue darting in and out of my mouth. I was too shocked to react, so I allowed her to continue – it didn't take long for me to get hard. After she fellated me – paying particular attention to the underside of my prick with the tip of her warm glorious tongue – swallowing every last drop of my hot semen she rose up to her feet, wiped her mouth, and picked up a book from one of her numerous bookshelves. Quite embarrassed, I quickly pulled up my trousers.

"Have you read this?"

"What is it?"

"It used to be my father's and his father's before that and so on and so on . . . It's a book of histories . . . London histories . . ."

I looked at the bedraggled leather-bound book, the title was indecipherable. It was the oldest book I had ever set eyes on, not that I had seen that many. I remember thinking it was probably the oldest book anyone had seen for that matter. She turned to me again, her eyes burying into my head, leaning forward.

"Do you know how many streets there are in London?"

"I would imagine a lot . . ."

"No one quite knows . . . It says so here . . ."

"But that's referring to the time it was written, surely?"

"If the book says it is . . . Then it is . . . Besides, I'm currently attempting to find out."

"How?"

"By walking them . . ."

"What do you mean?"

"I'm walking every street in London."

"Impossible . . . How?"

"I've devised a route, it's going to take me a number of years . . . Possibly the whole of my life . . . Here look at this . . ."

She passed me her A4 notepad. I didn't open it. It was heavy; it felt like it was being used for something important.

"In there are all the streets I have already walked down . . . Names, dates, times."

"You can't possibly . . ."

"I can."

"I've got to be going"

"Okay."

"By the way . . ."

"What?"

"What's your name?"

"Irina."

"Matt Hamilton, goodbye."

"Goodbye . . ."

[...]

The next time I bumped into Irina I was walking north along Bridport Place. It was my second attempt at my walk. The sun was hanging low in the cloudless sky above North-East London. I was feeling down, Arsenal had been beaten the previous evening – an outrageous penalty decision that tainted the whole game. The streets were mildly busy, just the usual suspects: school children, workers, homeless hooded figures and pigeons. She was sitting on a bench reading a book, her A4 notepad by her side, twiddling her pen in her mouth, her lips naturally red. I can't remember the title of the book because as soon as she saw me she put it back in her bag to greet me.

"Hullo Matt."

"Hullo Irina"

"Do you want to come to my flat?"

"Yes."

She was wearing a short denim skirt. I followed her back down Bridport Place towards her flat on Penn Street. As soon as we got inside she pulled up her denim skirt and bent herself over the kitchen table before pulling her black thong to one side with her right hand. I noticed faint freckles on her calves and a red blemish around the top of her hips from her thong. She wiggled her arse seductively.

"Fuck me here like this!"

She threw a ribbed condom at me. After exactly three minutes and forty eight seconds I came. The clock on the wall above our heads struck mid-day. She let out a short moan as the last of her own frantic finger-strokes on and around her clitoris brought her to a climax. After this she calmly stood up and pulled down her denim skirt like nothing had happened. I pulled off the condom and threw it into the bin by the table. She smiled at me. I pulled up my trousers as she put on the kettle to make us both a cup of earl grey tea. I didn't really know what to say.

"How is the walking going?"
"I walked one hundred and thirty streets this very morning. I documented every step . . . The signs, the windows, the people, the shops…"

She took the pot of tea into her small living room. She delicately poured us both a cup. My cup was red, hers was blue. It tasted good. After finishing the earl grey she got up and reached for the old book again. She held it like it was a fragile object in a box or something. Again she turned slowly to look at me.

"Do you know that the average family unit in London owns between two and three cars, any one household? Why do they need so many? Most have at least one four-wheel drive, which is just sickening . . ."

"That book . . ."

"Yes?"

"When was it published?"

"I don't know."

"Are you reading this information from the book?"

"Yes."

"But the motorcar wasn't invented when that book first went to print . . . Surely?"

"Well, I don't know about that..."

"Who's the book by? Who wrote it? Let me see?"

"I don't know, I don't know...NO!"

"Let me have a look!"

"Have you finished your tea?"

"Yes, I have."

"Then I would like you to leave . . ."

"But . . ."

"Now."

[...]

I was walking, having recently marvelled at the Dutch-gabled neo-Jacobean delights of De Beauvoir Square behind De Beauvoir Road, towards Mortimer Road heading south onto the very tip of my curve when I began to think about Irina again. I was also thinking about that book on her shelf and how I could steal it from her. I had never stolen anything before, not even as a teenager. I paused momentarily to observe a dead pigeon on the pavement – the crows had had its eyes and innards. I continued my stroll after kicking the limp feral carcass into the gutter by a grid. Three weeks had slipped by since we were last together, in that time I had filled two A4 notebooks of my own with comments and observations gathered from my walking. I was building a psychogeography of my own. Just what I was going to do with these extensive jottings I didn't know, all I knew was that I had to get my hands on that book. She was standing by a burnt-out stolen scooter on Enfield Road. We nodded at each other and immediately walked in silence towards her flat. As usual the flat smelt of earl grey tea. She took off all her clothes.

"Slap me."

"Where?"

"Here . . ."

I slapped her hard across her face. She must have liked it because she fell, squirming like an eel out of water, in obvious ecstasy on to the cold wooden floor. She opened her legs incredibly wide with all the insouciance of a seasoned porn star. I stared at her dark pubic hair. It wasn't red. It had been shaved into a thin strip. She looked magnificent.

"Come here . . ."

She threw another ribbed condom at me. I pulled my trousers down and rammed it into her. She felt hot inside. It was hard to control myself. She leant her head forward to have a look at it pumping in and out; the corner of her top lip began to curl.

"Pull that thing off . . . On my tits . . . On my tits . . ."

I pulled the condom off just in time and shot it all over her small, pert breasts. She rubbed it in with her hands, licking each finger when she'd finished. We lay breathless for a short moment and then got up off the floor to put our clothes back on. We sat next to each other on her blue sofa. I still had the discarded ribbed condom in my hand, so I slipped it into my pocket when she wasn't looking.

"Where's that book?"

"What book?"

"The old book . . . With all the answers you insist on showing me each time I'm here . . ."

"Oh, that thing . . ."

"Yes, that thing. . ."

"Oh, it's over there. . . On the shelf . . ."

"May I have a look?"

"No."

"Why not?"

"Because you can't."

"But that's ludicrous . . ."

"I know . . . But that's just the way it is . . . Why don't I read to you from it instead?"

"Okay."

She walked over to the book on the shelf. I should have grabbed the book from her. Have it over with once and for all. I didn't understand what had come over me. It was like I was possessed. She opened it at a random page:

'"*There are currently over 24,000 people living under the streets of London in a complicated labyrinth of tunnels and networks; a dark warren of subterranean passageways, disused bunkers and unfinished train routes. Couples, loners, cats, dogs, families and rats share this subterranean wilderness with the dust and the filth and the misery. Many have spent their entire lives down there, bathed in the unremitting blackness. Rumour has it there is a tunnel running the full length of Kingsland Road in the East of the city giving shelter and comfort to over 3,000 vagrants, most of whom have been marginalised, expelled and pushed out of overcrowded communities up above them in the outside world. Electricity is taken direct from the main grid. Most of these subterranean London vagrants arrived from far-flung corners of the globe but race isn't a concern of theirs down below the streets of London. They have no need for it down there in the depths. The majority of us don't know, or care for that matter, that they exist. No concrete evidence has been found confirming this underground community deep beneath Kingsland Road, but just ask any of the numerous traders around Dalston market, or the petty pan-handlers eking out meagre existences on this most historical of London highways above the pitiful, disparate bunker-dwellers below and they'll tell you of its very being. It is common knowledge around these parts . . .*'"

"Fascinating."

"Yes it is. I love Kingsland Road. I love it because everyone else hates it."

"It stinks of rotting meat most days…"

I watched as she put the book back into its place on the shelf. She looked truly wonderful; yet I had no feelings for her whatsoever. But that book, I had feelings for that book all right. I wanted that book more that I had wanted anything in my entire life and I was prepared to do anything I could to get my hands on it. It was more a question of when I got hold of it than how.

[...]

One week later, towards the end of my walk, on Whiston Street in the crepuscular light and the dizzying glare of the rush-hour traffic I decided the next time I saw Irina I would kill her and get that book. It wasn't that long before I saw her, she was crossing Kingsland Road, weaving, A4 notepad clutched to her breast, through the heavy impatient traffic without a care in the world. She set her piercing eyes on me immediately. I walked over to her. Back in her flat she stripped and handed me some rope.

"Tie me up face down on my bed and then fuck me hard in the arse . . ."

I did just as I was instructed to do, tying her hands up at the wrist behind her back. Again, I put on a ribbed condom. I pulled her arse towards me, gripping the soft malleable pale flesh of each arse-cheek. She nodded towards a bottle of Johnson's baby oil on the bedside table next to a well-thumbed book called *Helen & Desire.* I squirted the oil in-between each mound of bouncing flesh and rubbed it liberally into her arse, slipping up a couple of fingers to the hilt without any problem. She wiggled like a fish on a hook gasping for air. I took out my fingers and positioned myself. I slipped it in at an obtuse angle so she could feel the full intensity of its length and girth. Her dark red hair fell onto her shoulders and the pillow below her hidden face. She literally screamed in shudders of obvious delight as I manically thrust it up her tight arse, pushing her head violently into the soft pillow. It didn't take me long to empty it up inside her. I pulled it out slowly. She fell into the duvet, sweat droplets forming on the arch of her back. I untied her and she got up to go to the bathroom. I dressed in silence, leaving the used condom on the bed, before walking back into the living room where she joined me a couple of minutes later. I noticed that her old book was on the coffee table and not in its usual place on the shelf.

"Some light reading?"

"What?"

"There . . . The book . . ."

"Oh that, I was reading from it earlier this morning . . ."

I wanted to hold it, to pick it up and indiscriminately flick through it. I wanted to own it, to bathe in its words. She picked it up and walked with it in her arms around the room.

"Do you want me to read to you from it again?"

"Yes, I do."

"I wouldn't have asked if I had a problem with it . . ."

"No . . . You wouldn't . . ."

I watched as she opened another page at random and began to read aloud:

"'No Londoner, or any other person for that matter, has ever walked on every street in this most ethereal of conurbations. Many have tried this mind-numbingly near-impossible task; all have failed miserably. It is said that whoever accomplishes this gargantuan endeavour will become London, will be London, will at once be filled with its histories, its wonders, its secrets, its lives and loves: its sour losses, its crimes, its triumphs, its decadence, its madness, its repetitive cruelties, its wondrous possibilities. This propitious human being will be its ebb and flow, its multitude, its very flesh and bone. This sole genius who, dare we even contemplate it, manages to walk its multitudinous streets in their sprawling entirety will be rightfully given sole possession of all the answers to every question ever asked; and until this day arrives – and it one day will – this book will continue to be written.'"

The rope was in my hands. She closed the book and took it back over to its shelf. I ran the coarse fibres through my fingers. She had a slender neck. It wouldn't take much effort on my part. I walked up behind her and before she could turn around or utter one syllable I twisted and wrapped the thick rope around her neck and began to pull as hard as I could. I remember the veins bulging in my arms. It didn't take that long to kill her and I was quite surprised at how easy and straightforward the whole process was. It was almost like she knew it was going to happen. She lay motionless on the floor by my feet, her face a cartoon-like purplish-blue; a dark angry bruise beginning to form around her cracked neck. I remember thinking she looked like a manikin that had been knocked over in a department store by a boisterous child – awkward and cold. I picked up the book from its place on the bookshelf. I remember a wave of pleasure shooting down my spine. The book felt soft and warm in my hands, the antiquarian leather caressing my sweaty palms. I picked up her A4 notepad and walked out of her flat after making one last cup of earl grey tea, relishing each delicious sip, hugging both of her prized possessions close to my chest. I was now the sole owner of the book and it was up to me to finish Irina's mission: I would walk the remaining streets until all London's knowledge was mine. But first I would read that book.

[...]

My flat was cold. I hadn't, it seemed, been spending that much time there. I took off my coat and placed the book and A4 notepad onto my coffee table. I went for a quick piss and returned to read the book. I was almost salivating at the prospect of the wonders contained inside. I plonked myself down in my favourite armchair and picked up the old, bedraggled book. I opened it, the first page was completely blank and so was the second . . . the third . . . the tenth . . . the fortieth, I frantically flicked through the entire book – it was completely empty, its frayed pages bare, bereft of any writing. I looked through the book again, in denial, but it was true, it was completely empty. The book, that book, that wondrous harbourer of wonder that should've been mine was nothing but an empty vessel, a sham, a lie, a prank, a witch's brew, a rotten piss-take. I looked at her A4 notepad and picked it up, I was afraid to open it, but I did; it read:

"'One day I will understand . . .'"

Over and over and over again; on every conceivable page; on every line; from front to back and back to front. I could have cried. But I didn't – I just slumped further into my favourite armchair and thought about that book. Irina was dead because of it. And I had killed her because of it. And there was nothing I could do about it. Everything I had done up to the roughly textured rope squeezing the life out of her, tightening around her poor, limp, weak neck had been orchestrated by myself for reasons that were beyond my comprehension – because of one article, one page of printed copy. Words, all I wanted were her words. I was a murderer, a killer, a freak because of them. I had ended the life of an individual and one day soon there would be a knock on my door and I would have to pay for it. And until that rat-a-tat-tat came I would continue to walk, I would continue to discover the magic that lies beneath each step I take. There was, and still is, nothing else left for me to do.

The Only Living Boy on Oxford Street

Aaron Farrington had been working in his new job now for twelve days. His new job? Not worth mentioning really, other than it involved holding a rather large, awkward, advertising placard for a ubiquitous high street sandwich chain on Oxford Street, all day long. Sweaty bacon rolls. Rain or shine. His cold, numb hand gripped onto the sign from nine in the morning until six in the evening, every single day – the yellow arrow above his head a constant reminder, an embarrassment. The people passing him by felt like a predatory swarm of wasps buzzing angrily under his nose. He felt like walking away every tortuous second, but he never did of course, he needed the money. Each day was the same: a blur of oblivious shapes, smells and voices. The same aching feet and shins, the same bitterly cold fingertips, the same loud music from the same loud shops – only the random gaggle of teenagers with nefarious intent, each gaggle more vociferous than the last, broke the relentless monotony. Each day felt like his castigation, his penance, his purgatory and hell. Except for her. Aaron Farrington's one simple ray of sunshine. She walked past Aaron Farrington twice, at the same time in each direction, every day. What does she do? Where does she go? Why doesn't she look at me? These were the only questions he asked. Other than the brief moment between the hours of one and two in the afternoon there was nothing else for him to do. He couldn't read because he found it hard to juggle both a book and his sign. Nobody ever stopped to chat, not even the homeless, so what was the point? He just looked down at his toes; the same thoughts floating pointlessly inside his head: the same longing for acknowledgement: her acknowledgement. Maybe I should just speak to her? Maybe I should at least make eye contact, smile even? Aaron Farrington had had enough. It was time for him to do something about it, he realised it was time to break the silence, to approach her, to bite the bullet and attempt some sort of conversation. Some form of human contact. Anything. He looked at the clock that hanged from the building opposite. It loomed above the hoards, a sinister reminder to all, a constant eye, ticking away the hours left to consume, it was three minutes to one. Soon she would be here. He looked up Oxford Street in the direction from which she always first approached and within one minute he noticed her walking along towards him, weaving through the crowds as if they weren't actually there.

Aaron Farrington's heart began to pound. What do I say? What do I say? What do I say? She was almost level with him. He just spoke; the words sounding feeble as they poured from his cold lips.

"Excuse me . . . Hullo . . ."

She looked at him as she walked. He tried to step forward but the wind from a passing bus knocked him off balance, causing him to stumble a little.

"I don't think so . . . Do you?"

Aaron Farrington looked down to his feet as she continued to walk past. His heart sank; there was nothing else left for him to do. He waited. He waited for her to return. He even waited in the vain hope that she would walk back with a smile and an apology. Just something. His feet aching; the oblivious masses blurring into one giant mess. A backdrop for her to walk onto. But she never did. Soon it was six in the evening and it was time for Aaron Farrington to hand back his large wooded albatross and take his bus back home. Ready to do the same the next day. Only this time Aaron Farrington knew he would never see her again.

Anon Takes a Lunch Break

My, look at you; you're a fine one, look at your coat. Look at your striking green hackle. You're proud aren't you? With your little swagger. Look at your beautiful coat shimmer in the light. It's so shiny. Come here, come here. I won't bite. Come on. Do you want a bit of my sandwich? I bet you do. Come closer, here you go, there you go. Oh, you're so cute. Go on. Go on eat the bread, the nice homemade bread. Go on. Hey! Hey! What's wrong? Why are you turning your nose up at my bread? Look. Look there it is. There! THERE! No, no, don't fly away, I didn't mean to startle you, it's just my bread that's all, yes that's it, just there, come back, that's it just there. Oh, here you are, here's some more, a nice soft bit without the crust. It was too hard for you wasn't it? There you go, nice and soft, you can't turn up your nose at that . . . There you go. Hey! Hey! What's wrong with my bread? Why won't you eat my homemade bread, my succulent bread? Okay, okay don't go. Here. Here have some of this brie if you don't like the bread. I can't believe you don't like my homemade bread; it only came out of my oven last night. As fresh as you can get . . . I thought you pigeons ate anything,

I thought you weren't fussy. Ha, the things I've seen you eating, my god: dog crap, puke, soggy tissues, even discarded nappies! What's wrong with my bread? Here then, if you don't like my bread, have some brie, good French brie. What! WHAT! It's there! THERE! What's wrong with that good chunk of fine French brie? You can't turn up your little nose at that too, can you? What's wrong with you? You're a pigeon; you're supposed to eat anything. There! There! Quick! QUICK! Now look, your friend's gone and eaten it. Right, one more bit of brie, good French brie, and then that's it. These are my sandwiches you know, my lunch, I make these everyday. Okay, there you go, just there by your gnarled, weather-beaten feet. There! THERE! What's wrong? Don't you like my good French brie? But why? You're so cute and little and funny. Okay then, okay. If you wont eat that how about this? Yes, yes it is, it is, it's roasted aubergine. Mmm, yes, you'll like this. I roasted it myself in fine extra virgin olive oil. Just last night. Organic too. There you go my little beauty, there you go little pigeon, feast on that, go on, go on, GO ON! See, now look, see your friend has gone and eaten it. Right, one more piece, just one more, this is my lunch don't you forget. I don't have to do this you know. Oh, but you're so cute, the way you nod your little head and blink, the way you dance in little courtship circles, you're so cute. Here have this other piece, I'll throw it just for you, so your nasty friend doesn't see. There. There, look. Look! Hey! Hey! Where are you going? Where are you going? Why are you walking over to him? Come back; come back to your roasted aubergine. Now look, your friend has just eaten it again. Hey! Where are you going? What are you walking over to him for? Chips! He's eating chips! I've got homemade bread, French brie and roasted aubergine for you. He's just got sweaty, greasy chips. No! No! What are you eating those chips for? What about my homemade bread? What about my French brie? What about my roasted aubergine? Chips? I don't do this for the hell of it you know. This is the only hour I get free all day. Oh, you have it so easy. You have it so easy. Flying, eating and fucking. That's it! That's all you have to do! If only you knew. If only you could understand how mundane my life is. I get up. I commute. I sit at my lousy desk all morning acting on orders like a drone; speaking with people I have nothing in common with. I feed the pigeons in my lunch hour and I smile. I go back to my desk. I sit at it all afternoon acting on more orders like a drone; speaking to more people I have nothing in common with. I commute back home. I bake bread. Good homemade bread that you don't like. I sleep. I wake. I make sandwiches. I start all over again. Oh, you have it so easy, so, so easy. All I offered you. This is my free hour. And you throw it all back in my face by eating his chips. His lousy, greasy, sweaty, disgusting chips.

On the Banks

The fish weren't biting, not that they ever did that much. Sometimes, just sometimes they would. But that wasn't the point: Gordon Maldon didn't fish the banks of the Regents Canal for sport. Mal – as he preferred to be called – fished out of pure boredom. He fished because he liked the two swans and the Canada geese that visited his spot each time he cast his line. He liked the way they moved, the two swans, and the fact that they never left each other's side, that they had each other and nothing else seemed to matter that much. Mal didn't like to waste bread, so he never fed them, he just fished. He never fished at weekends though, only on weekdays whenever he called in sick from work. Mal didn't like work; his office was large and lifeless. His colleagues bored him. Mal didn't much like fish either, he thought them stupid and knew very little about them – he liked it that way. But, oh yes, he liked the Canada geese, they always seemed to be smiling, they seemed content. Each time he sat on his chair and cast out his rod they would welcome him in gaggles and Mal would wave at them. And later his two elegant swans would appear and cast their large eyes upwards at him. Mal would smile at them. They would hang around for a while and then gracefully glide away to carry on their intimate romance elsewhere. Mal liked that. Mal was from Islington, but he preferred to fish in Hackney on the stretch of canal below De Beauvoir Town – it was something to do with the way the light reflected off the numerous tower blocks' windows, causing it to shimmer across each ripple of the canal's murky depths. So there he sat in his favourite spot and along came the two swans. Mal looked up from his line and smiled. Work was far away – the City and the rest of London just didn't exist. Mal looked one of the swans in the eye, it was the female. The swan looked at Mal without blinking and then elegantly turned her long slender neck back over to her partner. Mal whistled – hoping that she would look back at him, but she never did. Then it happened. Without a sound. The swan shuddered. Her neck dropped violently. And then another shudder; as quick as the first. A tiny pap in the air a split second before a small splash in the water. The swan let out a sound not too dissimilar to a baby crying in the night or two foxes mating. In any case it was loud; the shrill caused Mal to jump. He watched: the swan lilting . . . And then slowly sinking . . . Half its bulk in the water . . .

A last gasp . . . A sad, sad lament . . . A large gaggle of Canada geese retreating in sonorous horror . . . The dead swan's mate staring . . . Dazed . . . Uncomprehending . . . Circling its partner . . . Leaving a chilling, almost ethereal pattern in the water as its legs paddled frantically beneath its white, stoic form. And then another pap and a splash, just by its side. Mal turned around – he saw them. They were sitting on a wall behind the cover of some trees Mal didn't know the name of; about fifteen meters away – airguns in hand. Mal didn't need to think about what to do next, he just ran towards the two teenagers with the air-guns. He was enraged. He wanted to kill them. The two teenagers saw him approach, giggled, then jumped from the wall and began to run. It was executed in perfect symmetry, as if planned and rehearsed countless times before, their little feet landing simultaneously on the wet grass. Mal picked up his pace and continued to follow.

"Hey! Hey! Murderers! Murderers! You little fuckers! Murderers! You killed my Swan! You killed my fucking Swan! Murderers! You! Hey! You! Murderers! You little fuckers! You little murdering fuckers!"

Mal chased them all the way to the edge of the De Beauvoir Estate. Each tower block loomed above – almost mockingly. Suddenly, the smaller of the two teenagers stopped, turned and took aim. He felt pain in his right ear, the blood trickled down his neck. Mal continued to run, the teenager began to falter and Mal gained ground, his ear stinging in the cold air. Mal was now a metre away, the young teenager began to flag some more. He lunged forward and grabbed the teenager by the back of the neck. The other, larger youth clambered up a wall separating the large housing estate from the towpath and the water's edge. Mal gripped the teenager hard; he yelped like a dog and threw his air-gun into the water as his accomplice jumped over the wall and out of sight.

"Why did you do it? Why did you fucking do it?"

"Dunno . . ."

"No, come on . . . Why did you do it? You! Why did you fucking do it? Why? Why? Just tell me . . ."

"All right man, all right. You're hurting me. Get off me, man . . . WE DONE IT 'COS WE'RE FUCKING BORED! BORED! BORED! FUCKING BORED! It was only a fucking swan anyway."

Gordon Maldon loosened his grip and slowly fell to his knees.

"You killed my fucking swan . . ."

"And you, mister, owe me money for a new gun . . ."

The teenager took a deep breath, wriggled himself free and ran. He ran, ran, ran as the blood continued to pour from Mal's ear.

Night Shift

It wasn't her fault. To be quite honest, it was the last thing she wanted to be doing. It was a means to an end, how she paid her way. It was what she did. But what else could a young, good-looking girl do? There was no one else to pay her through university. There were no rich parents to fill her pockets with beans. So she spent her evenings in The Northgate – a rather respectable gastropub in North-East London. She was a barmaid there. Well, what else did you think she was? A stripper? No chance, she had far too much respect for such degrading idiocy. She hated her job at The Northgate. Okay, her colleagues, a couple of them at least, she could just about stomach – it was the clientele she vehemently hated. Every last stinking one of them. Quite frankly, they bored her senseless, they were imbeciles who just drank and blathered, drank and blathered. She wasn't interested in what they did for a living. Media this, media that, photography this, photography that. She didn't give a flying fuck about their phoney lives.

But who pays for all this? She never saw cash being handed

over: the marked-up bottles of fizz and plonk were always paid for by credit card – always. Never old-fashioned cash, of course. Nothing was owned outright: it was all rented, it was all to be paid back at a later date. Whenever that was. This didn't stop them though, the blatherskites. Nothing was real. This is what got to her, this is what ate away at her as she polished glasses and served expensive bottles of wine to the them. The fact that all these people looked the same, sounded the same, dressed the same; they all had the same haircuts, the same tastes in music and literature – they all looked like their mothers had been fucked by the same lousy father. They all regurgitated the same old drivel: holidays in Budapest, boyfriend trouble, girlfriend hassle, fashion, nightclubs, Shoreditch, money, jobs and house prices, house prices, house-fucking-prices. It was all they talked about, and they talked about it loudly. It was too much, she didn't need it – it wasn't what she wanted in her life. She just wanted to finish university and move on to a better life. These people bored her to long tears of rage. They always had done and they always would do and they would never be any the wiser

Anyone else wouldn't bother, she knew that much, anyone else would just do their job, take their money at the end of the evening, maybe stay for a staff drink and then leave. But this whole work-for-a-pittance thing ate away at her like a canker. She simply couldn't ignore it. All she wanted was some money and to pass her finals – and nothing else.

He walked into The Northgate at around 9.30pm. She instantly recognised him as a man who probably hated his species. He had that look about him, surly, brooding; it was natural, of course, not contrived. He was young-looking for his age and always had been. Some people are naturally like that too, she thought. She picked up a glass and began to wipe it. He was probably in his late forties, yet looked mid-thirties. He was dressed head to toe in black – in clothes that fitted him well. They looked bespoke, tailored, well-made. He had large, lived-a-life, bags under his blue eyes, both hanging from his face like two buffed-up oyster shells; yet, his face was smooth, the supple skin clean, the blue eyes piercing and clear – Rasputin-like she immediately thought. He looked like he hadn't smiled in a very long time, possibly never. He walked over to her. She put the glass down.

"Hullo . . ."

The man was well spoken.

"Hullo."

"Right, yes, well, could I have a large glass of your Tempranillo?"

"Yes."

She poured the wine slowly and with aplomb – if there was something she did take seriously in that place it was the wine. Not a drop was spilt.

"That'll be £5.75, please."

Er, well, I'd rather have it for free if you don't mind . . ."

"Pardon?"

"May I have this glass, this large glass of fine Spanish Tempranillo, for free please?"

"Er, well, I, er, I don't . . ."

"Come on, surely you can give me this glass for free?"

"Well, I don't know if I can, the bottles might be marked . . ."

For a brief nanosecond it looked like he was about to crack a smile. She began to laugh. He didn't.

"Marked? Hogwash . . . Come on, why not? It's just one heavily marked-up in price glass of red wine . . ."

"Yes, and I know that. But, you see, the principle foundation at hand here, well, is that you purchase the goods before taking them away . . ."

"So, how about, just this once, we discard convention and you kindly give me this fine glass of wine for free . . ."

"Okay then . . ."

She didn't have to give it much thought. It was the simplest of things. She just handed him the glass of Tempranillo like it was the most ordinary thing in the world. To be honest, she didn't much care. What, in the grand scheme of things, did one lousy glass of Tempranillo matter? It was hardly going to change the world as we know it. It was nothing. It would never be missed. Ever. She watched him drink the wine. He poured it into his gullet like it was ice-cold water on a sweltering summer afternoon – although it wasn't, was it? She had never quite seen red wine drunk in such a manner before. She was even sure it wasn't poured into the gut like this at Dionysian festivals in Ancient Greece. She watched him. It took him two quick gulps to finish the glass. He turned to her.

"Right, are you going to quit your job now and come along with me?"

"What?"

"Are you going to quit this ridiculous job and come with me?"

She didn't have to think twice.

"Okay then."

She walked out with him. Without even mentioning her erratic decision to her boss. She didn't care. She followed him out of the door, after grabbing her coat, bag and a large packet of sea salt and balsamic vinegar crisps. She didn't look back.

"Where are you taking me?"

"Soho, of course . . ."

[...]

Soho was teeming with drunks and revellers. The entrance to the bar was awash in garish neon – the music pumping out onto the pavement from the large speakers by the door was loud and European. She followed him towards the bar. She could feel the eyes digging into the back of her head, her breasts, her arse and thighs from the numerous men sitting on stools – dirty stares, filthy stares, lecherous and unnatural stares. Each of the men, she noticed as she hopped onto a stool, were of a certain age and possessed a certain rakish look about them. They obviously wanted her to know that they were available, yet most, she noticed, were married and the whole bar smelt of rotting flesh, of decaying meat. The men looked her up and down, pools of saliva pouring from their lips. Suddenly more bespoke suits and plum accents entered the room from a door towards the back of the bar. At first she wondered why such well-heeled men should frequent such a tawdry little bar in the first place – it soon became apparent.

The woman followed and walked into the room wearing next to

nothing – there was an immediate raucous, boozy cheer from the gathered men. The rotting flesh peeled from the woman's tired stinking bones. The woman certainly could move, she thought that much. But the stench emanating from her was repugnant. Lumps of putrefying flesh plopped onto the bar as she twirled and gyrated. The men leant forward to get better looks. The decomposing woman was the sole reason the men were there. The woman, her blackened, mouldy skin flaking from her thighs, turned to the men with a cocky smile, her gums spewing puss between the little stumps where her teeth should have been.

"Who's going to be the first to buy this lady a drink then, cunties? I'm thir-sty boys . . ."

The men jostled and clambered in front of each other at the bar, vying to be the first to buy the woman a drink.

"GREAT SHOW, SWEET CHEEKS!"

Hollered a tall skinny man at the back. It was a free-for-all. A large, perspiring fat man was the first to purchase the woman a drink. She immediately walked over and plonked her stinking arse cheeks onto his lap. Brown and fetid bodily waste spilt from her tail end onto the man's trousers as her mouldering bladder and bowels began to tear under the stress and motion. The other men whooped and cheered. The pungent aroma filled the bar. She watched. The fat man bounced her up and down on his knee – just as he probably did with his grandchildren at the weekend. He was having the time of his life.

The man whom she had followed into the bar ordered two glasses of champagne – and this time he paid. She sipped from the glass, it was better than working, she felt that much. Again, he gulped down his drink.

"Not bad . . . A bottle, I think . . ."

She shrugged as he signalled to the fusty barmaid. He bought a bottle, paying for it from a large wad of notes rolled up Cockney wide boy style. He peeled out two fifty pound notes, again paying for the champagne. When she drank it she thought it tasted of fizzy strawberries. She had never touched expensive champagne before. She even began to forget where she was, the hovering stench and the flesh-splattered walls disappearing into a foggy cloud of bubbling bliss. The champagne went straight to her head – and for a fleeting moment she actually felt like she was enjoying herself. She didn't even mind the viscous rivers of puss and bile at her feet.

"So, when do you want to start?"

"Pardon?"

"When do you want to start, here, working for me?"

"What? Here?"

"Yes, here, when do you want to start? It's good money, and you can drink champagne every night if you want to . . . Some of my girls clear four hundred a night in tips alone . . . Think about it . . ."

"What?"

"Think about it, anything should be better than that wretched pub you were working in earlier . . ."

It was a strange feeling, the one that stuck in her like a childhood memory, of a time gone by, another world. She felt happy. She felt that whatever she said next was entirely a decision of her own making, her own reckoning. She turned to the man, his eyes didn't look as blue as they once did, his skin was leathery and textured now, old and stale.

"I'll give you an answer when I've finished this . . ."

She pointed to the bottle of expensive champagne. He smiled. She thought it looked mawkish and forced. Out of place. For a moment she thought his skin was about to crack, his oyster-shell eyes squinting like an old man reading a bus timetable or a headline in a broadsheet newspaper. Either way, not properly being able to focus. She sipped the champagne with relish. She had to admit that it certainly tasted good.

She watched the woman fall from the fat man's knees and onto the floor in a filthy heap of steaming shit, bile, guts and rancid flesh. The woman began to laugh; slowly and awkwardly the fat man got up off his chair and began to fondle the woman, grabbing and groping what was left of her flabby, soiled breasts. The rich, drunken crowd of men chanted and roared in paroxysms of delight. She didn't care. She had a decision to make. She drank and listened to the man without even listening to him, nodding when she felt she should. Even the loud European music couldn't touch her – its heavy, monotonous vibrations floating by her ears like freak feathers from a pigeon just startled by a cat. Soon the bottle of champagne was empty and upon her very last sip she turned to her host and said:

"No."

With this, she simply hopped off her stool and walked into the Soho night, without once looking back, just like she had done earlier. He didn't follow her. She knew he would find someone else – they always did. The narrow streets were awash with people – most were drunken and loud. She walked through them like they didn't exist, without a care in the world – apparitions all around her – and she felt safe in the knowledge that she would never work in a bar again.

The Fat Slubberdegullion

The first time this happened to me I attempted to write it down in an A4 notebook some time later. When I read it back to myself I ripped it up in disgust, worried that someone may have been reading it over my shoulder – something was missing and my mind wasn't right. I used a HB pencil. This is the second time this has happened to me now, not that this sort of thing should happen at all, and it is the second time I have tried to write it all down, only this time I used a laptop. A Sony VAIO VGN-A517. But still, as I read it back to myself, something rankles deep within. I may have to delete it. Maybe something needs to be drastically changed in my life.

Most of the time David Davis carried on his back a thick stench of body odour that could clear a packed room, or a train carriage even, it was that potent. David Davis didn't care though; he didn't much like people anyway. The further they stayed away from him the better as far as he was concerned. I first experienced the stench when he joined me in the photocopying room on my first day at work. I was full of a cold but could still detect his presence; his thick body odour seeping into me through my pores, seeping into my hair and clothes. I didn't mind though, there are worse things in life than the smell of another human being. His first words to me were:

"Watch them in there mate, a bunch of shifty fuckers . . ."

And then he left the room, his thick stench trailing behind him like a shadow on a late summer's evening. All I could do was laugh and I instantly thought nothing of it, having heard this sort of thing on numerous occasions. So I continued to photocopy the invoices I had been given, as the warm fog from his odour enveloped me completely.

Three days later I was back in the photocopying room and so was David Davis. This time he said to me:

"Have they got to you yet? Have they? Have they started to eat you from the inside out? Like a parasite in the gut? Like a fat worm in the dietary tracts? Have they?"

I left it at that. I didn't want to answer him. The smell, the putrefying odour that filled every space, hanging in the room like a phantom, like something rotten, thick like the stench of a raw salmon fillet left in a fridge that didn't quite work properly over a number of weeks. A sick type of smell. Cell deterioration. Collapse. Decay. I thought nothing of his words. It was only work. It, and he, meant nothing to me. I've spent my entire life photocopying other people's meaningless information. I've had to listen to them day in and day out, their nonsense, their earnest beliefs, their orders – why on earth should I listen to David Davis? He was obviously mad and had obviously been there too long, complete and utter cabin fever, lived with his mother and obviously slept with prostitutes, that sort of thing.

The following Monday I was minding my own business in the photocopying room as per usual. Monday always being a busy photocopying day everywhere. David Davis walked in. He was in a terrible state. His fat, flabby flesh hung off him like lard discarded from meat. Yellow, pale, dribbling with sweat. The fat slubberdegullion stood over me, breathing his disgusting black-death breath all over me.

"Why are you still here? Can't you see they're all useless, all pointless? With their expensive clothes, their transparent banter, their office affairs . . . Don't you just want to see them all dead?"

I looked him up and down. He looked dead himself. Like he'd been dead a long time; skin mouldering, falling from him, sloppy deposits by his feet like rancid butter, smeared down his cheap C&A suit and onto the floor, humming like warm hair-grease on an unwashed pillow, reacting continually with the oxygen around him. I had to speak.

"Why do you keep saying these things to me?"

"What things?"

"These warnings . . ."

"Because you're just like me. You see what I see . . ."

"And what do I see?"

"Nothing but bile . . ."

"Bile?"

"The filth . . ."

"Filth?"

"This . . . The workplace . . . A breeding ground for filth and rottenness . . ."

"It pays the rent."

". . ."

"I said it pays the rent . . ."

". . ."

"I said . . ."

"Kill them . . ."

"Pardon?"

"Kill them . . ."

And with this David Davis left the photocopying room. The next day I called in sick. I didn't want to see him again. I didn't want to find out what he wanted to tell me next. The man was clearly a twit. Completely fried. Something should have been done about him; he should've been removed from the office at once. But he wasn't.

I avoided work for a whole week before I had to return. I walked to my desk and switched on my PC to check my emails, I shuddered: all of them were from David Davis. I opened twelve, one after the other, each of them displaying the same crude message:

'Kill them.'

I didn't open the rest. I had to tell someone about this immediately. I began to feel sick. I walked towards my Line Manager's office. It was the first time I'd ever knocked on his door without him having summoned me there himself. He looked surprised when I walked in. Shocked even.

"What's happened?"

"I think, I think I'm being stalked . . ."

"Pardon?"

"David Davis has been stalking me . . . Loitering around the photocopying room whenever I'm there . . . Sending me emails . . . I'll show you . . ."

"Okay."

We walked over to my desk. I clicked the mouse hastily. My inbox was completely empty. All of David Davis' emails had been deleted. I looked around the open-plan office; most of my colleagues were sitting in front of their computer screens oblivious to our presence. David Davis was nowhere to be seen.

"But . . . I . . . This morning, they were there . . . They were there . . . He told me to kill them."

"Pardon?"

"Kill them."

"Kill who?"

"Them, you, me, everyone . . ."

"Are you sure you're okay?"

"Of course I'm fucking sure I'm okay . . ."

"Well, David Davis isn't even in today . . . He's in Copenhagen . . . You know, he's one of our most valued employees, you know that don't you? . . . His record is second to none, respected by almost everyone. I can't see how, or why for that matter, David Davis, one of our most valued employees, would ever want to stalk anyone, let alone you. He just wouldn't want to jeopardise his career in that way. It's just absurd . . ."

"But I saw those emails, I saw them . . ."

"Do you feel you need to go home?"

"I don't know what I feel . . ."

I took three more weeks off work, requesting that the company doctor diagnose a sorry bout of nervous exhaustion. He complied and signed the necessary forms for the entire three weeks. I did nothing more than sleep, eat and watch kung fu films. I didn't think about work and I certainly didn't think about David Davis. By the end of the third week I was feeling much better – enough to have visited my local gastropub a few times for a lunch of fresh oysters washed down with a couple of pints of good warm Guinness. I was starting to feel quite normal again.

The step back to work wasn't a large step at all and most people seemed quite pleased to see me back. The meeting with my Line Manager also went rather well: he too seemed pleased to see me and greeted me with a standing handshake and a warm smile.

"Glad to have you back."

"It's a pleasure."

"I always knew you were a team player deep down."

"You're right there, boss."

I took a deep breath and approached the photocopying room with a newfound vim in each step, taking a large stack of invoices with me. With each new step it felt like I was bouncing, or walking on air, although it was most probably the new pair of Clarks I had bought for the occasion. I was alone and content, with just the hum of the photocopying machines to keep me company. Suddenly the door began to creak open and I didn't need to guess who it could be. David Davis walked into the room, followed by a stench quite unlike no other: rotting corpses instantly sprung to mind, hundreds of them, all piled up on top of each other, flies buzzing around them, putrefying yellow/brown/snot-green puss oozing out from every conceivable orifice. I started to gag. He inched closer to me, the stench thickening, wrapping itself all around me.

"So, you've come back to do it then?"

"What are you talking about?"

"You've come back to kill them all? Like I asked you to?"

"No . . . No, I haven't. What are you talking about? Are you mad?"

"Don't they make you sick? The things they say? The repetitive conversations? The boring lives? The things they do? The duplicitous friendships? The dreary banter? The blind acceptance of it all?"

"I don't know what you're talking about."

"I'm talking about this . . ."

"What?"

"Work of course . . ."

"What about it?"

"How corrosive it is . . . How it eats you inside out, turns you into an automaton . . . A zombie."

"David, if you don't leave me alone I'm going to have to complain about you again. I've already done this once, I don't really want to go through this again."

By now the pong was unbearable. I wanted to run but something had nailed me to the spot; I couldn't move. Transfixed. David Davis looked at me, but not in his usual pathetic little way. He glared at me with more ferocity than I could ever imagine and I could immediately see into him – I could see what he was thinking. At first I wanted to laugh but soon the first image flashed into my mind instantly and all thoughts of crap Stephen King novels were obliterated: the Sales Team had been locked into a room, all the men had had their throats cut and the women had been tied up. Some were screaming and some were strangely silent. Blood was dripping from the walls and desks, splattered across flat-screen monitors and screensavers. David Davis stood over them with the knife in his right had and a gun in the left, he was rubbing his burgeoning crotch with it whilst looking over to young Michelle from Accounts (all of 19 and still living with her parents and pet Labrador, Alfie, somewhere in Enfield, North London) who'd just announced she'd become engaged to Steve (an aspiring club DJ), her boyfriend of one year, that very day.

The second image was just as explicit. My Line Manager was sitting at his desk with a large knitting needle protruding out from his left eye-socket (where the eye had disappeared to was anyone's guess). His stomach had been ripped clean open and red gut and purple entrails had been poured quite deliberately onto his desk, his files, laptop and the numerous pictures of his wife (Judy) and two adoring daughters (Molly and Bella) quite deliberately. Most chilling of all though was the bloody smile that had been cut into his face with a pair of scissors (now on the floor by his feet, open, red with his blood). Snip. Snip. Snip.

The third and final image forced me to vomit into the nearest waste-paper basket, drenching my Clarks with a thick viscous gloop. It was at that moment David Davis started to laugh. What I then saw was quite beyond comprehension: a figure was crouching over a body, struggling with something. It soon became apparent that the figure was trying to remove a head from a body with a largish knife that had become blunt with the stabbing, gashing and killing. The motionless body was a colleague of mine, Tom Tinder, whom I quite liked and often drank with in the local pub during lunch. His body was punctured with knife entry wounds. The figure struggled with his head, jabbing the blunt instrument in at the neck, hacking mercilessly at tube and bone. Little by little Tom's head began to work free from the rest of his limp, rather dead body. A short burst of thick red blood shot up momentarily. The figure yanked the head, stretching the last piece of skin and sinew like an elastic band. Soon the point of elasticity was reached and the head was wrenched, in its entirety, from the bulk. Thick gunk-like blood dribbled and oozed from the open wound. Slowly the head was lifted aloft as the figure began to rise and turn towards me. The face of the figure was manic and covered in blood, the red, thick droplets dripping from his chin. I watched the gooey droplet form and, yet again, slowly relent to gravity's pull – and it was at the exact moment the droplet was pulled from the victim's chin, to start its downwards trajectory towards the cold floor, that I realised who the figure I had been looking at was.

[...]

You know how these stories end. The upshot was that the job obviously wasn't right for me and it was obvious to all that I should leave immediately. So I thanked David Davis there and then on the spot, as he continued to glare at me, and walked out of the photocopying room, grabbing my coat and bag from my desk along the way, and out of that wretched building forever.

I never found out what happened to David Davis. For three weeks after the events I have just described I scrutinised the local *Evening Standard* each day and night, half expecting some dreadful news: a horrid workforce massacre. The same one I had seen, but it didn't happen and I soon got bored, like most people do, with the *Evening Standard* and began to occupy my mind with other things.

I'm working in another office now, doing pretty much the same things I used to do in my old job, and the job before that. Luckily no one seems to emit the rancid odour David Davis used to do, and nobody has decided to stalk me yet. It's not a bad job actually, like my old one I get to do a lot of photocopying, which gives me a lot of time to myself. I try not to think about work. I try not to think about most things really.

Footfalls

Martin Hack – a simple office assistant – walked to work each morning. He had been working six days a week for the last three months. He felt quite fortunate in that respect, not the hours he was working of course, but the fact that he was able to walk there. He wasn't aware of one single colleague who could say they too walked to work each morning. This being central London it was quite a rare occurrence – tales of tubes and trains and buses and near death experiences on mountain bikes and Bromptons were the order of the day by the photocopiers each morning. Martin Hack felt quite unique if he thought about it – which he often did. He always stuck to the same route, not that he was a creature of habit, it was just the quickest way that's all. He had checked other possibilities and was now almost 99% sure that he had found the quickest, most interesting route. He nearly always saw the same people walking along: the same faces at bus stops, the same old ladies waiting by the post office, the same besuited gentlemen entering tube station entrances with glum faces, heads buzzing with figures. Walking to work was as much part of Martin Hack's life as the air he breathed.

Monday 9.03 am.

Martin Hack stepped across the zebra crossing by the building site. It had been a heavy weekend, what with combining work on Saturday with a friend's birthday at which everyone had drunk far too much leaving Martin Hack comatose for most of Sunday. And being the age he was he was still feeling fuzzy with the hangover. They seemed to hang over him these days like a sodden, irritating heavy blanket, hard to budge as its weight seeps further into the chafing skin. The headaches never bothered him, nor did the excruciating nausea that bubbled and fermented in his flabby stomach like warm wallpaper paste in a bucket. It was the malapropisms that bothered Martin Hack and there was nothing he could do about it, as the harder he tried to think before speaking, the more tongue-tied he became. It was better for him to hide in a corner and get on with things alone and in silence. The words didn't come easy and if they did, they were mostly in the wrong order and context. He didn't much care about it these days – not openly anyhow.

The two voices reverberated across the street from atop the highest reaches of the towering scaffold. It caused two young pigeons to take flight from an overlooking window ledge.

"Just put the fucking fucker right there you fucking little cunt."

"All right you fat twat, keep your fucking bald head on your shoulders . . ."

"Listen cunt, put them fucking there you fucking arsewipe . . ."

"Fuckoff dickhead . . ."

"You fuckoff . . ."

"Twat."

"Cunt."

Martin Hack had to smile, a flutter, a little paroxysm of delight. The trappings of puerility had never actually left him. He was now 37 and industrial British plosives still bought a wry smile to his face come rain or shine.

Tuesday 9.03 am.

Martin Hack stepped across the zebra crossing by the building site. It was an inclement morning, but this slight matter didn't concern him. His mind was occupied with images from a book he had been reading the previous evening about the First World War. It wasn't the deaths that bothered him, but the smells, the horrid stench he imagined that must have lingered above the trenches like an invisible, obfuscating wall which closed in around each condemned man like the walls of a prison cell. The odour of war – especially that war – must have been nightmarish thought Martin Hack as rain began to fill the air. For once he was actually quite glad he led the life he did and, dare he think it, he was feeling quite content to be working where he was. This was an odd feeling: Martin Hack had never before felt lucky. The word was a stranger to him. He wore it uncomfortably, taking it off as soon as he could like an ill-fitting suit at a wedding reception. But this particular morning he wore his newfound luck with pride. And why shouldn't he? Martin Hack was an ordinary man, he deserved a bit of luck. He instantly began to quicken his pace. It hit him hard, like it had fallen from the sky above. Their voices unsympathetic, threatening and cockney.

"What have I fucking told you, you cunting fool?"

"What was that you prick?"

"You, you knob . . ."

"Don't give me all that bollocks . . ."

"You can fuck right off you fucking lag . . ."

"And you can put that in the right place you fucking nonce."

Martin Hack looked up towards the scaffold. The bald-headed man, who towered above his workmate, threw a trowel at him. It missed but the initial intent was quite nefarious. Martin Hack looked away.

Wednesday 9.03 am.

Martin Hack stepped across the zebra crossing by the building site. He possessed a beaming smile across his face – he was even whistling some made-up ditty, which was something he never usually did that much. Last night he had met someone. Nothing had happened, but they liked each other, he was sure of that. They had exchanged phone numbers during a pub conversation: Martin Hack was watching his beloved Chelsea play in the Champions League but had been momentarily distracted by her looks and charm. She was big and buxom, just how he liked them. Both had promised to text each other before the weekend. Things were looking up for Martin Hack and he half expected it this time. The voices tumbled down from the scaffold, he was ready for them.

"Aw, come on you fucking twat, what did I say? What did I fucking say?"

"I dunno . . ."

"What do you mean you don't fucking know?"

"I dunno . . ."

"What?"

"I dunno what the fuck you're fucking talking about, I've done every-fucking-thing you've fucking asked me to do you, twat, and still you cunt me off all the time . . ."

"Listen, shithead, put them fucking there, like I've told you…"

"Where?"

"There you slag, fucking there!"

The laughter from Martin Hack's mouth echoed across the street, he was sure the two workmen were looking down at him, but he didn't look up to check if his intuition was correct. They were arguing but he didn't care. He didn't have a care in the world. Each footfall towards his mundane office was a pleasure. And Martin Hack was happy in the knowledge that not everyone could say that.

Thursday 9.03 am.

Martin Hack stepped across the zebra crossing by the building site. He was thinking about what to say in his text message and when he should actually send it. Today? This afternoon? Late Friday? Never? He had stopped reading the book about the First World War – and, to be quite honest, had not given it much thought as to why he had. But the reason was obvious: Martin Hack was alive and he had never felt as resplendent. If the words pouring from the scaffold were rain, it was a murky downpour that could not touch him.

"Right, I'll fucking swing for you, you cunt. Are you fucking winding me up or something?"

"What've I done? What've I done?"

"What do you mean what've you done? You've done fuck all that's what you've done . . ."

"I have . . ."

"You fucking haven't you fucking lousy shite . . ."

"I have . . ."

"You cunting haven't . . ."

Martin Hack looked up at the scaffold. The bald-headed man was wielding a half metre long tube of scaffold at his workmate. For a fleeting moment Martin Hack thought he was about to witness a vicious assault. It didn't happen of course, the bald headed man walked away, his incredulity worn like a red cloak around his broad shoulders. Martin Hack continued at pace, still thinking about his future text message.

Friday 9.03 am.

Martin Hack stepped across the zebra crossing by the building site. He was holding his mobile phone in his hand, which, if he cared to admit, was odd behaviour, as his mobile was usually kept well hidden in his rucksack and if ever it rang he would usually choose not to answer it, denying the sound emanating from him was his. He had sent the text message the previous evening. He couldn't wait much longer. He was eagerly awaiting a reply. The voices startled Martin Hack, as shrill and arbitrary as any phone call.

"For fuck's sake you blind cunt, not there – there! – you fucking halfwit . . ."

"What, you dick? . . ."

"You fucking know . . ."

"No, I fucking don't . . ."

"Yes you fucking . . . Right, what exactly is your fucking problem?

"As I keep saying, I haven't got a problem . . ."

"Yes you fucking have . . ."

"I'm just doing my job, what you tell me . . ."

"You don't fucking listen, you cunt . . . If you don't get . . ."

"Get what?"

"If you don't get it right from tomorrow then you're off this site . . ."

"Then you'll fucking fire me . . ."

"And then I'll fucking lamp you one right in the fucking kipper, you mug . . ."

The bald headed man grabbed his work-mate by the throat. The work-mate went red in the cheeks. Then white. Then blue. The bald headed man then dropped his work-mate and stood over him, leering. Martin Hack hung back a little, slowing his step while anticipating a savage full-blown attack. But it never happened, the bald headed man walked away, leaving his work-mate wheezing on the floor. Mort Hack turned back to his mobile, hoping for a response.

Saturday 9.03 am.

Martin Hack stepped across the zebra crossing by the building site. He was happy, she had replied and they had both arranged to meet the following Wednesday. It was the happiest Martin Hack had felt in a very long time. He was so ecstatic he didn't notice how quiet the street was. Two old ladies blocked his path.

"Ooh, it happened yesterday at around 4 O'clock, police and ambulances everywhere, flashing lights, a right old racket . . ."

"Where did he fall from?"

"Right up there love, at the very top, must've been a horrible sight, they had to close the road for an hour . . ."

"Poor devil, who was he?"

"One of the workmen, Mary said it was the tall bald one . . ."

"Who?"

You know, always in the café at 2 o'clock eating egg and chips."

"Poor devil . . ."

"Police don't know whether he fell or was pushed, so Maggie at the launderette told me . . ."

"Really?"

"Really!"

"Do you think the press will be here?"

"Should think so . . . It's already in the locals . . ."

"I hope so . . . We haven't had the cameras here since that shooting at the Post Office . . ."

"No, don't suppose we have . . ."

Martin Hack walked by the two old ladies. A chill trickled slowly down his spine. He immediately thought about the book he had stopped reading, vowing that he should pick it up again that evening after he had finished at the office. It was going to be a long day.

Searching for Amy

Naturally, on the bright sunny day he was knocked down, Karl Dobson didn't see the bus approaching before it hit, sending him and his snazzy green Brompton sprawling across Tottenham Court Road. Naturally, Karl Dobson's mind was on other things. What they were he cannot quite recall. What he can remember, however, was the number of people who walked by as if he didn't exist – there may have been people watching, but he didn't notice. As if the sight of a man lying flat out on the warm bitumen was nothing but a minor obstacle on the way to bigger, and more interesting, things. His shin was sodden with blood and the driver of the bus that hit him – which had momentarily stopped at his side – was shouting something he could not comprehend. It could just as easily have been a somewhat concerned: Are you alright, son? Just as much as a disgruntled: Why don't you look where you're bloody going, you mindless clown? The hand gesticulations were the same whatever was being said. He got the message in the end. Quite dazed he looked around and noticed more pigeons were taking an interest in his embarrassing predicament than people.

As he lay there, little by little, the acute pain began to spread upwards from his shin to his thigh, hip, arm and fingertips – it felt like warm treacle spiked with rusty razor blades coursing through his veins. He stared at the multitudes passing him by; he looked into each grey, hurried face before he saw her approaching: a man swinging a walking stick violently without a care in the world, two skaters both wearing black and white checked slip-on Vans, a sad women dressed head-to-toe in black including hair and make-up, a young man with a red scar on his cheek, seven Russian builders (at least they sounded Russian to Karl Dobson as he lay rubbing his shin) eating McDonald's (he could smell the fat) while gabbling to each other in their native tongue, numerous other cyclists mostly riding Bromptons in an assortment of snazzy colours, endless white vans that all seemed to be blaring the same radio station as the last, a homeless man on crutches muttering to himself, a young man carrying a guitar in a case (who Karl Dobson thought was a Pete Doherty although he was probably mistaken) and then the young woman in the green coat.

"Are you alright?"

"Er, no – I think I've cut my leg. It's all gashed, I can't move it hardly, or bend it much."

"Who did it?"

"A bus, but he's gone. Can you believe that? I think the passengers started to complain. So he just started up the engine and whoosh, away he went. Isn't that illegal?"

"Most things are in this city. What's your name?"

"Karl. What's yours?"

"Amy."

"Pleased to meet you Amy. I like your coat."

"Thanks."

Karl Dobson tried to get up to his feet – he wanted to know if he was taller than her – but could only manage to sit himself up onto the curb. Amy sat beside him.

"Listen, do you want me to phone for an ambulance? Or the Police?"

"No, no, no, I should be fine in a minute. The pain's clearing. Really."

"Are you sure? I mean, you really shouldn't . . ."

"It's alright. I'll walk. Where's my bike by the way?"

"Oh, it's over there. Do you want me to fetch it for you?"

"If you could . . ."

Karl Dobson watched as Amy walked over to his battered snazzy green Brompton. Although the bike seemed a little tattered and torn it was still in working order, but he wasn't thinking about the state his snazzy green Brompton was in at that particular moment as, for the first time in his life, Karl Dobson had fallen in love. It was an odd situation to have found himself in: ordinarily he didn't believe in love at first sight, but he was willing to make exceptions for Amy. She wheeled the bicycle back over.

"Why did you stop to help me?"

"Because you looked in pain. You still do."

"No one else even noticed me. No one else even knew I was here. At least that's how it felt. And if they did, they certainly didn't care. Why did you stop?"

"I dunno. I generally wouldn't, to be quite honest. But I'm on my way to work."

"What do you do?"

"I'm a PA to an old, esteemed academic. I work at his flat in Soho. In his study. He's horrible, sleazy, stares at me all the time, lingers."

"So why do you work for him then?"

"Like everyone else, I have bills to pay. I suppose stopping to help you was a diversion. It meant I didn't have to think about where I was heading, just for that moment. You know?"

"Yeah."

The pain began to dissipate. Karl Dobson looked up at Amy and slowly rose to his feet. He felt taller, but he was not entirely sure. His shin hurt, but he didn't let it show. He could have hated London, his job, his flat, his life at that moment, but he never did. How could he have done? He was completely and utterly enraptured by her. The way her green coat hung awkwardly from her slender, hunched shoulders, the way she tapped her feet, the way she bit her nails and stood mawkishly – her entire weight on one foot like a cat sitting in a puddle. The smell of her. Her voice. How could Karl Dobson hate his miserable life at that precise moment?

"Well, you're standing."

"Yes."

Karl Dobson looked into Amy's dark eyes. He tried to hold her gaze like leading men did in the films he had seen, but she looked away.

"So, are you sure you're okay?"

"Well, yes, I'll, um, survive."

Karl Dobson watched as a large white van trundled by; its sound drowning out something Amy said.

"..."

"What?"

"Eh?."

"Er. Nothing."

"..."

Karl Dobson tried one more time to hold Amy's gaze, but it was no use, she looked nervously over her shoulder.

"Well, I suppose I'd better get to work."

"Yes, so shall I somehow."

"Are you, can you . . . ?"

"No, I'll walk. My leg, you know, it hurts."

"Yes, yes. I know. Okay then, er, Karl."

"Amy."

"I hope you feel much better."

"Yes, yes, Amy. I'm sure I'll be fine."

"Right then."

"Yeah, right then."

"Goodbye."

"Goodbye."

Amy walked away and headed up towards Soho. Soon she was engulfed by the endless tumult, the constant marching of the crowd. Karl Dobson picked up his green Brompton; it no longer seemed as snazzy as it once did. He pushed it along, walking with irregular limps, towards his office. The front wheel was buckled and it, like his shin, would need to be repaired before he could cycle to work again.

Within two weeks he was back on his green Brompton, but he was'nt cycling to work. Karl Dobson was cycling around Soho – as he had been for the last three days. He was searching for Amy. Just a glimpse would be enough. He cycled up Dean Street past The French House and The Colony Club, he cycled down Frith Street past the gallery, and he took a lunch break in Soho Square with all the other office workers, drunks and media types – all the while looking for a green coat amongst the throng. The pigeons crowded around his feet waiting for crumbs to drop from his brie and grape baguette. The next day he took yet another day off from work and continued his search, not one inch of Soho did he miss, from 8:30 in the morning until 7:00 in the evening searching for Amy. But he never found her.

In fact, Karl Dobson is still, to this day, searching for Amy. You can see him most days. He does not work at his office anymore – he lost his job a long time ago. Today he spends his time cycling the Soho streets, avoiding the buses, on his not-so-snazzy-anymore-snot-green Brompton. And deep down, deep beneath the dreary hustle and bustle, the fumes, the grey faces, the everyday humdrum trivialities of London Karl Dobson knows that he'll never find Amy again – because like a leaf that falls from a tree, any trace is soon swept away by the wind.

Mon Amie

Everyone needs somewhere to hide; everyone needs that moment away from the masses, the rabble, away from, well, everything. It's just the way we are. It manifests itself, this most human of desires, in many ways. You hear of people hiding in libraries, in dull marriages, in piles of never-ending paperwork, on the battlefield, in books that don't make sense, in one-night stands, abroad and at sea – it just so happened that I chose to lose myself in my local public house. I didn't even have the inclination to find an interesting one. There's a simple logic behind it really: I love to drink. It keeps me going. It's what I do best, if I'm honest. I can't help it, I'm useless at everything else life has thrown at me. But, it's my problem and I've just got to deal with it. It's better not to involve a second party – too many complications that way. So I deal with it alone, every morning, hung-over, when I have to get up for work, the alarm stabbing my head. I hate my work with an intense passion that is hard to describe at the best of times, but with that heavy cloud of the night before hanging over me, it's most intolerable. But what else do you do in my position? You drink, that's what you do.

It's easy; it doesn't take much of a decision to remove your hard-earned money from the nearest cash machine, most of the time it doesn't feel like yours anyway. You just simply spend, spend, spend – every last penny on booze. It's the easiest thing in the world.

I'm not going to tell you my name. That doesn't interest you. I am superfluous to your life. I am ordinary, ten-a-penny, ubiquitous. You've seen me, and countless others, so many times before. We mean nothing to you. So what's the point in telling me this? I hear you ask. Well, I'll tell you . . .

I had been drinking a long time and it had been a particularly long night. I was, of course, drunk. Or "rather squiffy" as the blatherskite with a plum accent on the stool to my left insisted on informing me at every given opportunity.

But what does one do when one's life is so mindnumbingly shite you need to hide away from it? That's it; you're starting to understand me now: you drink, of course, and you drink with relish and you don't really give a fuck who's sitting by your side drinking with you. You see? Everyone's superfluous to a degree. So I drank and I listened and I hated myself that one infinitesimal bit more – and that's a word you can't say whilst drunk. Try it. So do you understand? Do you realise how I have ended up here?

I am an ordinary man. I wear ill-fitting suits to work – mostly bought from Marks & Spencer, I own one Hugo Boss suit, but I don't wear it that much these days as my ever-expanding paunch seems to have outgrown it. I get the Tube every day. I take orders. I eat bland sandwiches from flashy food chains, between 1 and 2 in the afternoon, with all the other city drones. I put up with the human beings beside me – who I ask the same questions every day. I go home in the evening never wanting to return. Then I start drinking. I drink until these thoughts are washed away and no longer exist. Surely you can understand that?

On this particular, rather drab, evening it was raining – a light greasy drizzle that soaked everything except the earth. Like I said, I seemed to be spectacularly drunk, to the extent that even in that state I wanted more. Work, dare I say it, was a distant memory. But this man with the posh accent, I just had to get away from him; he was a constant reminder to just how much, and to such a lousy degree, I had failed. It was easy really.

"I'm pissed, I've got to go . . ."

"My good man, allow me the ease of another . . ."

"Sorry . . . But, fuck off . . ."

I walked out of the pub. I feared he wanted me for reasons I had never experienced before. The fresh air hit me like a drunk waking up from the night before. It didn't take me that long to hear it. It came from the foliage by my feet near an alleyway. It was a noise I wasn't that familiar with, although I was pretty sure it was something feral, I knew that much. I uneasily crouched down to investigate and it was then that I saw her: an injured baby pigeon lying on her side. I immediately looked up to where she may have fallen from, but there was no sign of any nest or worried mother. She must have been dumped there. She was in a horrible state, her tatterdemalion wings barely able to move. Even the presence of a large drunken human looming over her didn't seem to cause her alarm. In fact, it was as if she was looking directly at me, her small, nervous eyes clicking shut every few seconds like the prying eye of a camera. She was looking up, her tiny feet motionless, still fluffy, her hackle not yet fully developed. She was quite beautiful and I remember thinking that she was the first baby pigeon I had ever set eyes on before. Not many people could say that – baby pigeons on the streets being quite a rarity in any part of the world. I knelt beside her and stroked her with the back of my finger, she quivered momentarily. I swayed and fell to her side, nearly crushing her; she whimpered a long feral scream of fear – fleetingly aware. I slowly lay down beside her. The earth was damp and cold, I didn't care. She actually turned her head. Her eyes clicked shut once more and then I heard it. Another rustle in the foliage; this time above me and to the left. I knew what it was immediately. My first instinct was to pick her up, to take her safely home, out of harm's way, to take care of her – but my rotten human scent would smother her, she'd be worthless, they'd hate her – that's what they say isn't it? There was nothing I could do. Everything blurred around me: the trees, the road, the houses. I heard it again. It was the three of us now. I looked for the cat,

I looked for its eyes, it was out there somewhere looking at us, weighing us up, waiting to pounce. There it was again, another rustle in the dark foliage, this time before us. The cat was crafty. It was encircling us, slowly, patiently, waiting expertly. It had all the time in the world. I shouted out, I wanted the cat to disappear but this was the big bad city, it had heard it all before. I envisaged it yawning at my feeble effort. I just wanted her to have a semblance of a chance in life. It didn't seem fair. The most vulnerable creatures; they don't understand, there's always something out there, lurking, waiting to chew them up and spit them out.

You see? There's nothing clever about this, that's all there is to it, this is all you'll get. Don't bother reading between the lines here, there's no fancy metaphor on these pages. This is face-value. Surface movement. Get it? We're not special. This isn't a life-changing story.

I searched for a glimpse of the cat – the eyes would surely give it away. The cat can't escape from this fact; they have to deal with it just as little Mon Amie has to deal with her frailties. I had to give her a name, she deserved something. Those large eyes were near, I could feel them. In turn it's what at once attracts and repels us; the beauty and ferocity of those eyes. Suddenly I saw the cat, I leapt up as quickly as I possibly could, which wasn't quick at all owing to my inebriated state, grabbing some loose earth in the process. In hindsight this was a rather silly move as I could have picked up anything: discarded needles and used condoms spring to mind. I threw the damp clumps of earth towards the cat. I felt bad, I genuinely like cats. Both eyes clicked shut, as large as an owl's, and with that it was gone. I turned to my poor Mon Amie, she was completely oblivious, fading. It wasn't a struggle for her, she knew no better. Who was I to her?

I was pretty sure that the cat wasn't going to return, but I couldn't just leave her there. Yet what good would come of me taking her home? I wouldn't remember a thing in the morning, it would be difficult, what with work, and besides, it would just ruin any chance she ever had of returning back to her nest. I sat myself back down beside her, the booze flowing through me like a murky gully of filth and wretchedness. I sighed – I distinctly remember this because directly after, within a nanosecond of this most natural exhalation happening, the cat pounced – and it pounced with venom. And as instantly as she had entered my life she was gone. I scrambled to my feet, I shouted and stammered, a dreadful caterwaul, but she had gone. Vanished, dragged into the deeper, dark undergrowth like a rag doll, a mere toy; a piece of meat to be devoured. Gone.

You see? I had my chance, I could have saved her, my poor Mon Amie, but I didn't, my mind was clouded with rot and mythology, old wives' tales. I could have simply picked her up, cupped her in my trembling hands and walked away with her, taken her to safety, but I didn't did I? I simply lay beside her like a drunken fool. Clueless, empty and ordinary.

I walked back onto the road in the knowledge that my entire life could be summed up in that one brief encounter: a series of missed chances, a spiral of miserable blunders, myriad mishandled moments: a bastion of inertia, of nothingness. I walked home, like I had done so many times before, I stopped off for a large kebab with extra hot chilli sauce. I was hungry.

But please, do not misconstrue me, like I said, you've seen me countless times before. I don't wear black, I don't want to kill myself or listen to bands like Joy Division. I work and drink, I look like everyone else you see. I consume and watch TV, read the newspapers, books, eat and sleep. One day I shall be gone and no one will remember me, and no one will care, because that's the way it should be and that's the way it's always been and will be. You see? I'm ordinary, my wings are clipped, and anyway, I have work in the morning. I have things to do. Stories such as these are meaningless.

John Barleycorn

Okay reader, you know, I'm not really interested in this newfangled culture of drinking – not that I'm particularly *old*fangled if you get my meaning. Maybe you don't, it doesn't matter. I'm not one for caring. I'm not one for brands or gimmicks either, you see, I'm just for the drinking. I once saw a group of people downing shots of Cream Egg-flavoured vodka – maybe you understand what I'm talking about now? You do. Good. You see, I take my drinking very seriously, as you should. And who am I? I'm John Barleycorn, a worker by trade, and I sit week in, week out in an office breathing regurgitated, chilled air. Accounts Department – that sort of everyday thing. I'm not what you could describe as "going places". I pay my bills each month, dream about winning the lottery yet never buy a ticket, watch crap reality TV shows and wish my life was better. I'm 38 years of age, which doesn't feel that old. I'm single too – and no, I'm not looking for a partner, I'm not looking for someone to share my life with. I'm just looking for a drink. A simple, alcoholic drink. So that's why I'm here, in my favourite pub, when I should be at work. Right about now, if I was sitting at my desk, I'd be thinking about sitting right here – so, I figure I must be doing something right if I am actually here and drinking. So what are these newfangled things that irk me so? Where do you want me to start? Ah, just wait a minute. Thanks my love. That was the barmaid bringing over my drink. I think she likes me as I never bother her with boring anecdotes about my boring life. I never stand at the bar trying to impress her, I'm not bothered if she doesn't know how much I earn. Ah, tastes like black cream. That's my Guinness, perfectly poured I might add. It's my first of the day and I'm going to savour each drop. I can't wait for my second. Ah, not too cold, just right. Extra Cold Guinness, that's one of the many things that irks me. Extra Cold? A serious drinker never takes his drink too cold; we leave that to the Americans. How else would I be able to taste the subtleties of these flavoursome roasted/burnt hops? It doesn't make sense to drink a drink so cold you can't even taste it. But enough of that. I have drinking to do – tastes even better knowing that I should be at work too, but I can't work today, I have things on my mind, I have serious thinking to do. I like the idea that a man can sit in a pub with his pint and his thoughts, just mulling things over, you know? There's something quite glorious in its simplicity. My father always said to me before he died:

"If you've got problems son, then take yourself for a drink and listen to them."

He was right, you know; then again, he was always right. Anyway, I don't want to get all maudlin on you. Where was I? Oh yes: newfangled. All these new brands and ways of drinking, these sugar-coated brews, these adverts on TV, in the magazines, I don't get it. If a man wants to drink, he'll drink. He doesn't need to be told what, when and where; I mean: it's bad enough being told we can't drink. Imagine that? What a barren life that would be. I ask you one question: drinking games? It's not a game. Just give me a pint. Just give me a drink to devour each wonderful drop alone. I don't need companions for such things, and I certainly don't play games with my booze. That's why I don't socialise with my colleagues at work, not that they ask me anymore. Each time they get together they buy each other drinks that look like something from a Roald Dahl story. It's just not my thing. I tell them to drink real ale and they look at me strangely – it's not my fault they don't care to understand the complicated thought and history that goes into a pint of well-crafted ale. Pah, drinking games. And don't even get me started on cigarettes: whoever suggested that a cigarette is the perfect complement to a pint needs their bloody head examining. Addicts the lot of them. Solitude is a drink's best friend – they compliment each other like a perfect marriage. Solitude and alcohol. Time alone to drink without trivial interruption. The last thing that I want is some stranger telling me all his problems whilst bathing me in a blue/grey cloud of wretched filth. Like I said, I want to savour each drop, I want to drink. In peace . . .

Ah reader, you're back. Sorry about that, I just needed a piss. It's funny, I was just thinking, most people can remember their first drink of alcohol. I can't. Not that I have a bad memory, it's just that it's always been there, like alcohol has always been part of me. My only real companion. You see, that's just the way I am. Like it or not. You can say I'm an alcoholic, I don't care. The people on the next table probably think I am too. I wish they'd leave. You see reader, it's the kind of drinkers on that table next to me I despise the most: with their ludicrously stacked Bloody

Mary, bottle of French red and their oh-we've-had-such-a-heavy-weekend routine that simply doesn't wash with me. I've been listening to them. I don't normally do this, but I had no other choice. They're the sort of couple, and you've seen them too, who can't help informing the whole bar of their ever-so-interesting lives. I've been listening to them on and off for the last half hour or so. They're the sort of couple you just can't escape – their superior voices reverberating all the way into the Gents. The new breed of drinker. The biggest of my newfangled hates. These despicable cretins, oh I've been listening to them all right, as they sip from their preposterous-looking Bloody Mary and over-sized glass of French red, holding them aloft between each staged taste like a trophy. Just drink the damn things and leave this public house immediately. Either that or move on to something a little more serious. Like a pint of bitter. Anyway, I don't want to cause a scene, but do you want to know what I overheard them saying just a moment ago? You do? Excellent.

Her: I thought Robbie Williams was amazing. A true professional.

Him: Yeah, that couldn't be said for that monstrosity of a human being Peter Doherty . . .

Her: What was he on?

Him: Scandalous. Left a bitter taste in my mouth he did. Does he not have the mental capacity to comprehend the absolute importance of that day? Just like we all did, giving up our own time to help Africa?

Her: And the artists as well . . . They took the time out to perform for Africa . . . To help the poor starving children . . . Their own time . . .

Him: And what did he do? He just came on stage and stumbled around, looking like he was on heroin . . .

Her: He probably was . . .

Him: Sickening . . .

Her: Completely. A disgrace to us all, those images were broadcast worldwide . . . I personally found it an insult, we had the decency to attend this important historical day, we held the common decency to raise awareness for this most worthwhile of causes just for Kate Moss's boyfriend to throw it all back in our faces . . .

Him: Does he not care about Africa?

Her: I doubt it?

Him: Me too . . .

Ah, but it gets better, dear reader, much better. Oh, but this Guinness is so good today, it tastes so good, like velvet pouring into me, lining my stomach like a good mother mollycoddling her child. Wiping the tears away. On to my fifth now. And those moronic cretins on the next table are on to their main course.

Her: Is that Rosemary on your potatoes?

Him: Yes, but a smidgeon too much . . .

Her: Very robust isn't it?

Him: Yes, but accompanied with a weak olive oil, such as used to dress these, it makes for a disappointing combination . . .

Her: Yes, I suppose potatoes need to be well dressed . . .

Him: Yes, it's imperative that they are, always . . .

Her: Well, my aubergine is simply divine, it's absorbed every flavour on my plate . . . This port jus is as rich, ah, and the Lamb is just . . . Just . . . Ah, I'm sorry, it's simply delectable, I'm lost for words . . . Is the new chef French? By the way, how's your blue fin?

Him: Well, the chef can't be French as it's sadly over-cooked . . .

I mean, blue fin should be rare, rare, doesn't the chef understand this? Blue fin tuna should be cooked rare, always. Any two-bit chef worth his salt knows that . . .

Her: You should go and speak to him . . .

Him: I should, shouldn't I?

Her: Yes.

Him: Or maybe we should never eat here again . . .

Her: That's a good idea . . . The wine list is too fussy anyway.

Him: Yes, too New World for my taste . . .

And on and on and on they prattle as I gulp from my glorious cup. And if only you were here right now to witness it – you'd be supping up too. I devour each drop. Cretins. Don't they know that the blue fin tuna is dropping in population at an alarming rate? Can't they eat in a restaurant? Why do they come here and disturb my thoughts? Why do they have to invade my life, spitting their drivel onto their plates? Reader, I just want to drink. I simply want to sit here and drink. I don't want to listen to their bile, their sorry, jumped-up, supercilious voices. Their self-righteous prattle. I want to feel every last drop of the beautiful elixir trickle down my awaiting gullet. I must drink more. I must drown out their words. I must extinguish their presence with another glass. I demand more booze. I don't care how much it takes. I'll drink all day and all night if I have to.

Her: Go on, ask that barmaid there.

Him: I will . . . Er, excuse me! I said EXCUSE ME!

Barmaid: Yes, may I help you?

Him: Well, yes you may, this blue fin is ruined, I can't eat it . . .

Barmaid: What's wrong with it, sir?

Him: It's over-cooked, that's what's wrong with it . . . Can you kindly inform the chef to sort me out another . . . And this time can you make sure it returns to me rare? Okay? I want it to taste like it has just been plucked from the Mediterranean this very day . . .

Barmaid: Yes, I'll see to it . . .

Her: Well done, that's how you get things done . . .

Him: Yes, it is rather, isn't it?

Her: Hey, what's higher than a knighthood?

Him: I honestly don't know . . . Why?

Her: Well, I was just thinking, that's what Sir Bob Geldof should get . . .

Him: Yes, you're quite right. That's another man who gets what he wants . . .

Reader, do you see what I mean? Do you see what I mean? This is what I have to put up with. What is this wretched place coming to? What is happening when a man can't have a quiet drink without interruption? I've been working so hard all my life; I've taken one lousy day off so that I can be alone with my thoughts and my drink, and now this aberration. So now I must drink more. They force me to do it. People like them, there on that table, next to me. Them. So now I must drink more. I must escape these doldrums, dear reader, and I must continue to drink and always drink because I'm John Barleycorn and it's what I do best and all this drinking must be done alone away from the confusion, away from all intruders, the part-timers who infiltrate the places I frequent.

Oh reader, please allow me this time alone now, this respite, please respect my wishes, please leave me where I am and do not tell a soul. Please leave me now, the chances are I'll still be here when you get back anyhow – and you won't have missed much. So leave me until then. In the meantime I'm drinking…

Gravestones

Charlie Bruen's feet were sore. Charlie Bruen was sore. It seemed he'd been walking all day long. He didn't like walking all day long. He didn't like walking full stop – he preferred taxis. But today he hadn't the money for such luxuries. So Charlie Bruen walked. In actual fact he'd only been walking for about fifteen minutes, but already the muscles felt like they were being slowly torn from his shins like meat from an over-roasted shank. He was winding himself through the crooked side-streets of Hoxton. The gherkin-like Swiss Re building towered over the fading Georgian/Victorian slums of Hoxton Market, glinting in the distance, like a beacon beckoning him onwards to Old Street, his destination. There was a distinct odour of fried meat in the air – meat of every description: dripping donner kebab, sizzling chicken nuggets, kidneys and offal emanating from Cooke's pie and mash shop, fatty processed burgers from various ephemeral takeaways littering the street. A large gaggle of schoolchildren disturbed the ambience. Just as he was about to cross the street to purchase a red apple – his favourite – from a street trader a familiar voice clattered behind him. Charlie Bruen turned immediately on his tired heels to find Pat Owen – an old friend – grinning back at him.

"Charlie . . ."

"Pat . . ."

"What are you doing here at this hour? You normally don't venture out until mid afternoon at the earliest . . ."

"I have business to attend to . . ."

"Oh, you do? Well then, allow me to buy you a drink in celebration . . ."

"Oh . . . Well . . . I . . . Shouldn't really . . ."

"Yes you should, for the road, you know . . ."

"Well, I . . . Go on . . . Okay then, just the one mind . . ."

"Good man . . . Good, good man . . ."

Charlie Bruen and Pat Owen walked into The Bacchus – a real spit-and-sawdust Hoxton affair with wallpaper and nicotine-stained paint peeling from the walls. The ceiling was literally dripping in age-old sweat and tears. The overweight barmaid poured both men a pint of warm bitter and two cheap whiskey chasers each – this constituted one drink by Pat Owen's inebriated standards. The warm Bitter tasted good and Charlie Bruen let it pour into him like only a seasoned drinker could. He felt he deserved it after such a brisk walk. He immediately ordered two more of the same – after the first round was sunk of course. Both men talked about nothing in particular with verve and bonhomie until Charlie Bruen finally bid farewell and continued on with his journey. With his stomach full of booze the walk didn't seem to bother him as much and he soon began to find a pleasant and accommodating rhythm in his step. Charlie turned onto Fanshaw Street and looked at the numerous pigeons nesting happily in a burnt out dilapidated building. Each bird seemed jovial and content. It seemed like a good life to Charlie Bruen. He carried on walking and soon bumped into Cam Stoppard. He was sitting alone on a bench whilst sipping from a can of Gold Label. The sight of him broke Charlie Bruen's thought: he was going to miss The Bacchus when it finally closed.[1]

"Cam . . ."

"Why, if it isn't Charlie Bruen . . ."

"Cam, what are you doing here? All alone . . . I thought you'd have been propping up the bar of The Macbeth by now? . . ."

"Nah . . . I needed some time alone, you know . . . To think. She's only gone and left me again . . . Fancy a drink?"

Cam Stoppard held up a can of Gold Label, it caught the sun creeping down through a gap in the clouds and twinkled like a little fairy light on a Christmas tree.

"Well . . . I shouldn't really . . . I have business to attend to . . .
"Is that so? Well business should never be attended to on an empty stomach, here drink this, come and sit with me . . ."
"I thought you wanted to be alone?"
"I can't let an old drinking partner walk by without a slurp of the good stuff, now, can I?"
"No, I suppose you can't . . ."

Charlie Bruen sat down next to Cam Stoppard on the bench and opened the warm, gleaming can of Gold Label he had been handed. It tasted like warm treacle. Both men began to chew the proverbial fat – they eagerly talked about Arsenal being knocked out of the Champions League the previous evening. Neither of them was happy about some of the referee's decisions on the night. Cam Stoppard vehemently proposed that there should be more "consistency" regarding certain recurring "flash points" in the game. Apparently Cam Stoppard thought the referee a "cunting disgrace" who deserved to be "shot, not once, but twice in the cunting knackers". Charlie Bruen nodded his head as old friends do. He couldn't help thinking that Cam Stoppard was speaking sense for once – he rarely did regarding football as the horses were his game. Charlie Bruen soon finished his can of warm Gold Label and promptly bid farewell. He carried on his long slog then hesitated momentarily and, instead of walking on ahead onto Pitfield Street as he should have done, he turned back onto Hoxton Market and walked into the nearest Ladbrokes. Charlie Bruen had been given a hot tip by Cam Stoppard and it was a chance he just couldn't ignore – everybody knew that's how Cam Stoppard was able to put food on the table of an evening. Charlie Bruen put five pounds – half his money – on the nose. "Burning Tiger" was a sure shot said Cam Stoppard between slurps. Charlie Bruen waited, Ladbrokes was jam-packed with the usual weary faces. "Burning Tiger" eventually came in fourth. Charlie Bruen cursed, realising that when a woman leaves a man like Cam Stoppard it's probably because his luck has run out on the horses. He continued his crooked, meandering journey. Soon Charlie Bruen arrived at his destination. His whole body ached, especially his tired and worn out shins. He walked up to the plush, modern, sparse reception and spoke softly to the sombre-looking lady behind the desk.

"Hullo . . ."

"Hullo . . ."

"Yes . . . My name's Charles Bruen . . . I'm here to see Maisy Simmonds . . ."

"Yes."

"Yes, I have an interview . . ."

"An interview . . . ?"

"Yes, an interview for Post Room Operative . . ."

"An interview for Post Room Operative with Maisy Simmonds?"

"Yes, that's right . . ."

"I'm afraid all interviews are finished for the day . . ."

"They are?"

"Yes, you're over two hours late Mr Bruen . . ."

"I am?"

"Yes . . ."

"Well, can't I be squeezed in? . . . I've travelled . . . Can't I come back tomorrow? The traffic was a nightmare on the way in, and I don't own a mobile so I couldn't contact you, and . . ."

"I'm afraid that's just not possible Mr Bruen . . ."

"Right."

"Goodbye, Mr Bruen . . ."

"Goodbye . . ."

Charlie Bruen walked slovenly out of the building and back onto Old Street – he wasn't quite sure if it was the alcohol or the rejection that was making him walk with such a dishevelled gait. He walked like this until he reached City Road and then headed south. Charlie Bruen convinced himself that it must have been the assortment of alcohol he'd consumed as, if he really put his mind to it, he didn't much want the job anyway. Suddenly he noticed he was outside Bunhill Fields. Charlie Bruen liked cemeteries, he always had. He couldn't tell anybody why he liked them; he'd never thought about it that deeply. He just knew he always had, as far back as he could remember. He immediately walked inside. He walked slowly around the grounds, looking at the various sarcophagi, observing the pathway and keeping off the grass whilst looking for an empty bench to sit on. Charlie Bruen needed to think. He also needed to rest his tired and dejected limbs. He stopped. A smallish gravestone caught his peripheral vision. It was a small unassuming gravestone sitting rather forlornly beside an extremely grand plinth. Charlie Bruen was happy that someone had left a jam-jar with four fading irises in it beneath the unpretentious little gravestone. He read its inscription:

Near by lie the remains of
the Poet-Painter
William Blake
1757-1827
and of his wife
Catherine Sophia
1762-1831

Who the hell is William Blake the poor little bleeder? Never been one for all that poetry. All these grand gravestones around and all he gets is this little slab of stone. But, still, at least he has some flowers. At least someone remembers him, doesn't matter how grand you are if no one remembers you. At least people remember him. Whoever he was all those years ago. But that's it, isn't it? That's the end. Everything is meaningless if it just comes to this. A gravestone off the City Road choking in bus fumes day and night. Nothing matters. Nothing. My life is meaningless unless I'm remembered. And I'm remembered. I'm Charlie Bruen. I do odd jobs for people. A jack of all trades. People respect me. That job doesn't matter. It's about making the most of now. And now work doesn't come into it. It never has. Who wants to waste their years working for the bigger man anyway? You never get anywhere, and neither do they. Just a bigger bloody bastard of a gravestone that's all. And who needs that when you're six feet under? I need a drink.

Mother and Son

Nothing much really happens in a small town like Dorking. Most inhabitants spend their entire working lives commuting to and from London each day, there's not much time for anything else. A dinner party here and there maybe, a bottle of expensive wine on Sunday with lunch, a warm ale in the local with friends chattering about house prices and crime in the inner-city – people trying to impress other people. That's about it really. The high-street is equally as uniform. Drab, but useful, shops, tea rooms, pubs, independent wine sellers and two ubiquitous food stores not a stone's throw from each other – both selling the same expensive goods, fresh of course, only wrapped and presented in different packaging. The people of Dorking spend their days eating and drinking. The continual trundle of traffic strangles the town as it ekes its way through the high-street like a choking snake. It seems each four-wheel-drive is headed elsewhere and nobody can cross the road and nobody seems to care. There's no time to stop in Dorking. The ants in the undergrowth live peacefully here – nobody notices them. The bored teenagers sit sipping from stolen cans of lager in black tatterdemalion hoods on street corners like gnarled crows perched on a branch oblivious to the disconcerting growls and glares from the previous generation – who used to booze hell knows where. It's a recirculation of boredom, folks. Lone tabby cats with loving owners strut along as cool as cucumbers thinking about the next merciless kill. Dogs on leads guided by owners look on enviously. The pigeons gorping down from the trees, window ledges and guttering, like old men with nothing to do, carry cleaner coats and hackles than your average feral – all is well in their world too. At night the foxes raid the town in pairs, scavenging from bins left out on doorsteps, eating from discarded fish and chip wrapping. Easy pickings really, cloaked by the warmth of the black night. If you listen carefully you can hear the foxes sniggering and guffawing at the "Fuk Yer Ban Tony" T-shirts hanging to dry overnight on the lines. The foxes like Dorking.

[...]

The mother and son come walking up the highstreet. They cut an awkward silhouette before the bright street and the blue sky hanging above. The son is dressed in black and the look of incredulity slapped across his face will take an age to remove. The mother bent double with shopping bags is thinking about pots of tea and afternoon television. The son is in his late twenties. The mother is fast approaching a septuagenarian stew of her own. The son's arms are waving erratically emphasising his point. The mother looks at her toes like she's counting each step home.

"No . . . No . . . No . . . Are you stupid mother? Are you utterly redundant? Are you?"

"Eh?"

"It's not Arthur Miller it's Henry Miller . . . Not Arthur but Henry . . ."

"Eh?."

"It's Henry Miller, not Arthur Miller . . . HEN-RY MILL-ER . . . H-E-N-R-Y . . ."

"Oh . . . I thought it was Arthur Miller . . . ?"

"IT WAS HENRY MILLER, YOU DUNCE . . ."

"Oh . . . Henry Miller . . . Not Arthur Miller . . . ?"

The mother and son headed homewards along the high-street and through the Dorking throngs oblivious to it. It seems it's going to be one of those days again.

No 38[2]

Keith Price had a face that bounced up and down with each step he made, the whole face, as if it wasn't really attached to his skull. It was once described – at a rather drunken office Christmas party – as like a rubber mask that had not been fastened on properly. This astute observation was made behind his back, not that Keith Price was bothered by the things people said about him – he didn't care. Keith Price took the No 38 bus from home to work and from work back home each day and had been doing this for the last sixteen years. He mostly always saw the same faces, heard the same conversations and sounds. Why is everyone else involved in important business and not me? It always seemed to be raining in the winter and too stuffy and hot in the summer. Keith Price had fallen in love with a passenger once; it took him three months to pluck up the courage to even smile at her. One day he finally made up his mind to speak to her, but she never got on the bus. She must have changed bus routes, he thought. He never saw her again. His days were always tedious from beginning to end. But today was different. Today a large black sports bag – that had been left, he presumed, by a previous passenger before he got on the bus – was sitting beside him. Keith Price didn't know what to do. Is it a bomb? Is it stuffed with money? Private things? Papers? Documents? For the last ten minutes Keith Price had been trying to attract the attention of the conductor. As usual the No 38 was stuck in traffic on the Essex Road. Keith Price was on his way home from his office, his dreary job, his monotonous processing of other people's information, he had been dreaming all day about the pork chop he was going to grill as soon as he got home and was quite numbly content – until the large black sports bag had appeared and ruined everything.

None of the other passengers – and the bus was full – seemed to have noticed the large black sports bag sitting next to him. Should he open it and peek inside? Should he take it home with him like it was his own? Should he shove it under the seat in front and forget its very existence? Keith Price didn't know what to do. He turned to look for the conductor. He had started to sweat a little on his forehead but had nothing to wipe it with other than his sleeve and wiping sweat from one's brow with the sleeve of anything was completely out of the question in Keith Price's book. Even in a situation like this. The conductor was in his usual spot by the stairs, arguing with a passenger about the dangers of leaning out of the back of the bus while hanging onto the pole between stops. The conductor was extremely angry and Keith Price immediately noticed that the passenger was unusually calm for such a scenario – by now the whole bus was looking over too. Maybe it's his bag? Maybe the passenger has left it? Maybe it is a bomb? Maybe that's why he's smiling? He's going to kill us all! Keith Price tried to attract the happy passenger's attention, he raised his arm and coughed – not wanting to cause too much of a scene. Look over here. Over here. What's in that bag? Why today? Why now? Why me? What's in that bag? What's in that bag? Why can't someone else deal with it? Why can't it just be collected? Surely someone must be missing their large black sports bag by now? Who owns this bag? Someone's got to own this bag? Keith Price could feel the sweat pouring from his awkward rubbery face. He suddenly jumped to his feet.

STOP THE BUS! STOP THE BUS! CONDUCTOR! CONDUCTOR! THERE IS A LARGE BLACK SPORTS

BAG ON THIS BUS AND I WANT TO GET OFF! STOP THE BUS! STOP THE BUS! IT COULD BE A BOMB! A BOMB! IT'S HIS! THAT MAN'S! THE MAN YOU ARE ARGUING WITH! HE'S LEFT A BOMB ON THE BUS! STOP THIS BUS! STOP THIS BUS!

Keith Price ran towards the back of the bus, passengers started to laugh, they had noticed his face comically bouncing up and down with each frantic step he took. Keith Price didn't care; he just wanted to get off the bus. He barged in between the conductor and passenger – both stared at him incredulously – and jumped from the moving bus, he stumbled and wobbled on impact with the hard, cold pavement, causing his whole body to tumble over onto his back and from the passenger's perspective, still seated and watching agog on the No 38, the whole scene looked just like a reluctant small child learning a forward roll for the very first time. Keith Price picked himself up off the pavement and straightened his rubbery face. He could hear laughter from a group of schoolchildren, he watched as the No 38 bus, containing the large black sports bag, left him behind and trundled along and out of sight up the Essex Road. Keith

Price was glad that he wasn't still sitting next to the rogue bag. Now he could go home in peace and eat his grilled pork chop.

The next morning while standing at his usual bus stop Keith Price purposely let the No 38 pass him by without a second thought. His face hung awkwardly from his skull. Keith Price stepped onto the No 73. It was a new bendybus. It was the first time Keith Price had used the No 73 in sixteen years.

Red Letter Day

Hugo Heinz graduated from Library School thirty-one years ago and in that time he has occupied the position of Arts and Humanities Librarian, at the University of Sussex in Brighton. This has been his one and only job. Only two colleagues ever got on the wrong side of him in all that time: Sheila Hole and Elaine Lowbottom – something to do with a library social evening he didn't attend. Admittedly, he often looked back over those long, tiring thirty-one years, whilst sitting at his desk and pondered just what the hell he had been doing. He knew he had worked hard, but other than that his mind was completely and utterly blank. A librarian, that's what he was. Nothing more, nothing less. Hugo Heinz was sitting at his untidy desk as usual on this particular day. He picked up the phone.

"Hugo Heinz speaking . . ."

"Hullo Hugo, it's Sandy . . ."

"Oh, hullo Sandy . . ."

"We need to see you immediately in my office . . ."

"We?"

"Yes, we'll explain in full when you arrive . . ."

"Oh, okay . . ."

Hugo Heinz finished his cold cup of earl grey and walked upstairs to Sandy Earl's office. He made no connection between the tea and Sandy Earl. He knocked on her door.

"Come in . . ."

Hugo Heinz walked in. Sandy Earl was sitting next to Jackie Moran, the head librarian. Both looked up from whatever they were looking at and stared at Hugo Heinz without breaking into a smile. He took a chair, quite sloppily, without being asked. Hugo Heinz did not notice who spoke to him first.

"Hullo Hugo . . ."

"Hullo . . ."

"There's been a written accusation . . ."

"A what? . . ."

"Well, this is quite delicate . . ."

"Really? . . ."

"Yes . . ."

"Well? . . ."

"Last Thursday, the 12th, we received an email accusing you of taking a packet of biscuits, Digestives, from the Staff Room."

"Oh . . ."

"Yes, without paying . . ."

"Oh . . ."

"This is quite a serious allegation, Hugo . . ."

"Oh . . ."

"Yes, a written accusation has to be taken quite seriously. In the strictest of confidence of course . . ."

"Oh . . ."

"Yes. Can you answer a few questions, Hugo? . . ."

"..."

"Hugo . . . ?"

"..."

"Hugo, are you okay?"

". . ."

Hugo Heinz was far from okay, he rose to his feet. His whole face boiled. It was an odd feeling. He realized he hadn't been in Sandy Earl's office that often. Its cold walls were completely foreign to him – in fact, many of his colleagues, after thirty-one long years, still remained complete and utter strangers. Hugo Heinz didn't know any of these people. He couldn't stop himself.

"Okay, you pair of prodigious panjandrum oiks! You sullied ultracrepidarian dullards! You blinkered bastions of myopia!"

"Pardon . . ."

"How dare . . ."

"You horrible, snivelling refuge of brimborion! You pair of wretched harlots! You common tawdry trulls! You pair of drones! You indolent pair of boiled toads! You slimy newts! Drongos! You plebeians! You perfumed blockheads! You despicable pair of snake-like eels! You dim dunderheads! You piffled pipsqueaks! You pointless buffoons! You moronic cretins! Imbeciles! Hodmandods! How dare you! How dare you! Thirty-one years! Thirty-one years and then this, this aberration, this scourge, this!"

"But Hugo . . ."

"Biscuits! Biscuits! You drag me here, you embarrass me here, over a packet of lousy biscuits!"

"But . . ."

"Pah!"

Hugo Heinz walked out of Sandy Earl's cold office without looking back. Not once did he look Jackie Moran in the eye. He took his bag and coat from his office. He walked through the library without acknowledging any of his colleagues. He walked towards the Literature Department, towards aisle 194 and his beloved Knut Hamsun. He took a copy of *Hunger* off the shelf and rapidly stuffed the book into his coat and continued walking out of the library. And did Hugo Heinz steal that packet of Digestives from the Staff Room that fateful day? No, of course he didn't, Hugo Heinz hates Digestives with an intense passion – he loves Knut Hamsun though, that much he can tell you. In all honesty, not that Hugo Heinz looks back all that often anymore, it was the happiest day of his entire thirty-one-year-long career.

The Rodent

They're all so clammy. They're all so sweaty. They're all so gnarled and cold. Who are they? Who do they belong to? All these outstretched hands. I don't know them. Why should I? I've never seen them before in my life. And I'm pretty sure my father hasn't either and he was alive for some considerable time – eighty-four years I think. Yeah, I think that's right, at least I hope that's right, I'll have to ask. He didn't do much with them though. I know that much. So here they all are. Here, accompanied by that infernal organ, they present themselves at my father's funeral. I wonder if he worked with some of them. I suppose if you spend over forty years working the same job you get to meet an awful lot of people. Or maybe you don't, maybe you just see the same dreary people day in, day out. Imagine that? Over forty years in one job. If I'm still working in forty years then I'll have failed. I won't even be in this country then. I'll be living in St Tropez. I can't even remember what he did, something to do with engines I think. Nothing that important. Look at them the way they sit, twiddling their thumbs, looking around the church for acknowledgement, for other faces that shouldn't be here. How can they be so brazen? Probably only here for the free food afterwards. All from my pocket. This should be my day. I was his eldest child. His precious first born. This should be my day, not theirs. Not my day in that way, oh no, even I'm not that selfish, but my day in the sense that I was his eldest daughter for goodness sake. Saying that, I've had to miss three very important meetings to be here today. Three. That's lot of my time. When you're working in *The Media* like I am, day in, day out, a trip up north – even for something as delicate as this – can take a massive chunk out of your work schedule. This whole affair is going to set me back. Of that much I'm sure. That reminds me, I must remember to text Miles. I must ring Georgina also, must prompt those figures for marketing. Tim must have all the correct demographics noted for this one, they've all got to be in place. Everything's got to be just right. I just haven't the time for all this. I should've been in attendance for those meetings. How ironic, eighty-four years and it had to be this month. Of all the months to kick the bucket, it had to be the most important of my working career. Ah, there's the vicar. Ha, no. Ha, it is. It's the very same vicar that used to teach me at Sunday school. He still looks the same. He moves a little slower now though. And he's hunched. How long has he been doing this? What's the point? I bet he doesn't get paid that much. What's the point? Staying in one place for the whole of your life. Never wanting to move. I couldn't wait to get out of this place. I'd never have been the success I am now if I hadn't moved away to London all those years ago – and now look at me, little old me the MD. Oh, if only these people knew how hard I've had to work to get myself to where I stand today. Head of all operations, overseeing every project we undertake no matter how large or small. I provide all solutions. Look at the vicar. How many of these has he done? How many of his friends has he buried? The same words, the same weathered faces. There's more to life than christenings, marriages and funerals. He's done it that many times he's just mumbling now – I can barely hear what he's saying. He's just going through the motions. I'm just so glad I chose my path, I'm so glad I'm a creative . . . What was that? There, there, by that man's feet! I just saw it! There it goes! A rat! A rat! A rat! It's a rat! Who brought a rat in? There it goes. What's it eating? Scraps. Scraps. Why hasn't anyone else noticed it? It's huge. Can't anyone see it? There, that horrible, rancid, grimy little scavenging rat? A rodent in the house of God! A dirty scavenging rodent! This is an aberration! What's going on here? This is just so tacky. Just so drab. At my own father's funeral too. Oh, why can't this just end? Why can't we all just go home? I need to call the office, I need to call my PA, and I need to know how these meetings went. Oh no! Oh no! It's coming over to me. That big filthy rat. It is, oh no! It's at my feet! Don't move! Don't move! Go away! Go away! Why has it sought me out? Why me? What have I done? I work in a clean office. I wear expensive clothes. I drive an Audi TT. I have taste and class. I can do as I please. Why this rat? Oh no! Oh no! It's looking at me, sniffing. It's looking at me. Oh no, it's nibbling at my Jimmy Choo's No! No! Keep calm. Do not cause a scene. People are looking over. Keep Calm. People are staring over. It'll go. The rat will go. What's that noise? What's that noise? It's my phone. I didn't turn it off – at my own father's funeral! What will people think? What will people think? Just get up like nothing has happened. Do not make eye contact with anyone. Just get up. That's it. Get up and walk down the aisle. Do not look at anyone. Especially her. Do not look at Sandra, at Daddy's little favourite, do not look at your little sister. That's it. Keep walking. Keep walking. You can answer the call outside. That's it. I can't believe this is happening to me. What will people think? I needed to make an impression. How did that scavenging rodent get into the church? Right. Breathe in. Fresh air. Answer the call. Anna Denver's phone. Hullo. Oh yes, hullo. What? No? What do you mean? They've all pulled out? All of them? No! No! They can't! Right, I'm on my way back. Right, I'm coming back. I can't let this happen. I can't let this fall through. But, but, but nothing. I'm not wanted here anyway. I specifically told you I needed to be at those meetings. I knew it. Tell them to get everything back onto the table. I'm driving back immediately.

The Wolf

He knew the difference between right and wrong alright; such ostensible opposites littered his daily life. Right was escaping work, lying on the same beach so many had dreamt of; occupying his happy mind with nothing, doing absolutely nothing, dreaming of nothing. Bliss. Waking up each pleasant morning to the sound of the sea lapping up against the warm sand, the simple realisation that he simply had nothing to do. Nothing.

And then he would just forget this momentary thought, let his mind wander, drift off in new directions, and turn over.

Wrong was her. Wrong were her large green eyes, the way they hung from her face, blinking, drawing him in. Wrong was her languid walk, her short bobbed hair, her little flat black shoes that reminded him of a ballet dancer's. Wrong was most definitely her wondrous body. Wrong was watching her each day, listening to her conversations on the telephone. Wrong was asking her out for that drink, wanting to spend more time with her, putting up with boring talk of her husband (Tim), the new house (early Victorian townhouse), the three cats (Jimmy, Misty, and Moomin), the two dogs (Rory and Charlie). Wrong was wanting her so much it hurt.

He knew it was wrong, all wrong, but just to be with her, if only sitting near her, catching that glimmer in her eyes, her scent, a slight touch of the hand, contact: all this felt so right. He liked wrong because of this; he always would, as long as she existed, as long as she was there, as long as she looked at him the way she had started to: ever-so-slightly, ever-so-delicately. Those large green eyes. A personal thing, something they both could recognise. And when she asked him for a drink a few weeks after their first together he knew that was wrong too. So they went for that second drink together: it felt so right for a start.

[...]

The first time they went for a drink they sat quite far apart across a large table in a ridiculous gastropub in Hammersmith. This time, in the same ridiculous gastropub (same staff still behind the bar, same music drifting from the speakers, same clientele, same dreary art on the walls) they sat closer together. Next to each other. It might have been nerves or pure unadulterated excitement but they began to drink; one after the other: whiskies, gins, wine, anything that helped to loosen their tongues, helped them to talk without inhibition. He inched closer to her with each sip. He began to place his hand, lightly, on her knee to help emphasize points he was making, she didn't mind that either. It was so wrong, he knew that much, but there was nothing he could do about it. Those huge, green eyes, the touch of his hand on her knee. It was what he wanted.

Soon they were both drunk. A happy, raucous drunk. Nothing like the confused garbling from most drinkers at the end of the night. The cold air hit them as they walked arm in arm out of the ridiculous gastropub and into the street. He had placed his arm around her immediately. She allowed him to do this without hesitation. Suddenly a pigeon landed on the railings to their left (he thought it strange a lone pigeon at such an hour), she let out a startled scream which in turn startled him which in turn startled the pigeon. When he asked her why she screamed she told him it was because she hated them with an intense passion, that there were too many of them, that they were useless, and even though he vehemently disagreed with every word she uttered on the subject he liked it, so he let it continue. He liked the fact that she hated pigeons and he loved them with all his heart. She asked him to take her to the other side of the road and sit with her by a bus stop. The road was quiet and only a stray dog crossed their path. They sat together at the bus stop for thirteen minutes, just talking, before he leaned over to kiss her. She allowed him. It felt good. Soon he found his hand creeping up her skirt and, in turn, her hands frantically undoing his belt buckle. Her skin was warm and smooth and he liked the soft breathing from her mouth on his ear.

They fucked for three minutes at the bus stop before the stray dog returned, sniffing around them, and then stopping dead in its tracks to stare right at him. It was a deep and penetrating glare, it unhinged him somewhat. He stopped, and asked her to get off him. She did. She asked him why. He pointed to the stray dog. She looked over her shoulder and screamed: It's a wolf! It's a wolf! The stray dog scampered. He told her that it wasn't a wolf but just a stray dog. She didn't believe him, convinced she had just seen a wolf at a bus stop on a quiet Hammersmith street. The more he tried to correct her the more she began to laugh. He knew her laughing should have annoyed him, but it didn't. He buckled his belt back up and she rearranged her underwear and skirt. A stray dog, she said, how ridiculous. Yes, he said, you're probably right. Knowing that she was wrong.

[...]

The next day, at work, he emailed her. He mentioned the wolf, hoping that this would ignite some flirtatious banter. It didn't. What wolf? She said. He replied immediately, explaining in detail, the wolf that was really a stray dog at the bus stop on the quiet Hammersmith street. I can't remember, she answered, I was drunk. All I can remember is sitting in that awful pub with you.

He didn't send her another email. He felt sad. Embarrassed. He began to think about that one thing that always seemed to occupy his mind in such moments of despair: the beach, his beach. If there was one place he wanted to be it was on that beach, doing nothing, thinking nothing, the sea lapping softly onto the warm sand. For once he was right about something.

Tale of an Idiot

Judd French was sitting at a small table in the Bricklayer's Arms, Shoreditch. He was drinking Belgium lager and sending various text messages on his new Nokia 6630 smartphone with 6x digital zoom, 1hr video recording and email with Quickoffice document viewers. He was waiting for Max Hargrade from *exploit* – a local web design company. Judd French dreamed of designing for them. Freelance of course. Admittedly, he was quite surprised that he'd got this far: a meeting with their head designer. Max Hargrade was at the top and Judd French wanted his tutelage. It could be said that Judd French was in awe of Max Hargrade – he never told anyone this though. Why should he? Judd French had walked into the Bricklayer's like he owned the joint; he was wearing a silver Adidas shell suit jacket over a brown, rather tatty, slim suit. A Ramones T-shirt poked through between its thin lapels. On his feet Judd French wore second-hand cowboy boots – his drainpipe trousers tucked in of course. A small pork-pie hat balanced precariously atop his asymmetric hairdo. Judd French was feeling good. A rather old man in a scruffy donkey-jacket walked over to him. The man was strange, he looked like a witch, his long hooked nose and chin near touching at the tips, his skin was cold-looking, as if that of a man already dead – although, rather contradictorily, he was calm personified, a saintly quiet. Judd French had never seen him in the Bricklayer's before.

"I notice you like gadgets young lad . . . Are you waiting for me?."

"Er, are you Max Hargrade?"

"No, I'm Len Mishking . . ."

"In that case I'm not waiting for you, man . . ."

"Well, maybe you are, maybe this is a blessing in disguise."

Len Mishking edged closer. A bit too close for comfort. Judd French detected a distinct aroma of boiled cabbage.

"Oh."

"Yes. You like gadgets I see . . . Well, I have guns . . ."

"Pardon?"

"I have guns . . . German Lugers . . ."

"I don't understand . . ."

"Guns, prints of guns, German ones . . . Lugers . . ."

"Oh . . ."

"Prints you can use on T-shirts . . . German Lugers on your chest, any colour, on any T-shirt, that would look sooooo good, don't you think?"

"Well, erm, no . . . I don't know . . . I'm waiting, I'm sorry, I'm waiting for a web designer . . ."

"A what?"

"A web designer. I'm one too. We move media. We push brands. We create solutions in space. We mould pixels. We create electronic art. Perpetually pushing all that is out there, you know? Like web-fuelled media communities . . . Transient but stable . . . I'm waiting to discuss business, if you don't mind."

"I know about web design . . . I'm flash like that . . . Geddit?"

"No . . ."

"Hey, what's your beef, man?"

"Do you mind if I just reply to this message?"

Judd French's Nokia 6630 smartphone, equipped with broadband technology, 1.3 megapixel camera sensor and 10 MB Internal Dynamic memory caught the light and dazzled momentarily.

"No, I'll wait."

Judd French, whilst pretending to send a text message, took a sly picture of Len Mishking. He then proceeded to send a joint message to all his acquaintances and colleagues – including the newly acquired portrait – that read:

'Hey cats, a real-life Shoreditch Twat.'

Judd French gained immediate inner-satisfaction. As Len Mishking looked at him ponderously Judd French pulled out a book.

"Do you mind?"
"No . . . No . . . A man should always read . . ."
"Yes . . ."

Judd French opened his Penguin Classics edition of Dostoevsky's *The Idiot* and thumbed through it feigning interest. Len Mishking leaned in even closer.

"Have you read Fyodor before?"

"Who?"

"Dostoevsky . . . The man whose book you have in your hands."

"No . . ."

"Hmmm . . ."

"I'm using his name as an image . . ."

"A what?"

"A web page, you know, the in-ter-net . . . The world wide web."

"Hmmm"

"Yes, I'm going to have a site that shows media clips of celebrities acting like fools in public . . . You subscribe to it . . . It's going to be called *Dostoevsky's Idiot Files*…"

"What?"

"Yeah, I mean those fools have got to be real idiots downloading idiots acting foolish in public, subscribing to that, I mean, if that's what the rabble want we'll serve it to them on a platter . . . You know, kerching! Anda-thank-you please!"

"So, you've never read Dostoevsky then?"

"No, never, don't read that much actually, too busy . . . Just surf and create . . ."

"Hmmm. Maybe you should . . ."

"As I said, not enough time . . . Hey, this is Shoreditch, and we're too busy creating . . ."

"Are you a holy fool?"

"Pardon?"

"Are you a holy fool?"

"Eh? How dare you!"

"It's a simple question . . ."

"Wholly fool! Wholly fool! How dare you! Have you ever heard of *Rumble Fish*?"

"The Film?"

"No, the website . . ."

"No, should I have?"

"I created that . . . It's *Sleaze Magazine* endorsed . . . Over 4,000 hits per DAY!"

"Right . . ."

"So, no, I'm not wholly a fool . . . I have created . . . How can I be? I am part of this . . ."

"Part of what?"

"Shoreditch . . ."

"Do you want a Luger then?"

"No . . . Leave me alone . . . I'm far too busy . . ."

"Okay . . ."

Judd French turned his back and continued to gaze into his Nokia 6630 with Multimedia Messaging (MMS), Hot Swap MultiMediaCard (MMC) and Data Transfer application whilst waiting for Max Hargrade. Len Mishking wandered back over to the bar, occasionally looking over at Judd French. Len Mishking possessed a grin so wide it parted his long hooked nose and chin, almost making his features hang in symmetry. The Bricklayer's began to fill up with punters and soon became crowded. Gaggles of Shoreditch types. Judd French continued to wait for Max Hargrade but he didn't turn up of course. Max Hargrade was far too busy.

Joe Blow

Who's Joe Blow?

Get me Joe Blow!

Get me the next Joe Blow!

Who's Joe Blow?

- Anonymous Proverb (Hollywood, California)

It was sweltering inside the library. It was sweltering outside the library too. There must be some semblance of a breeze somewhere. This is what Joe Blow was thinking it seemed. Joe Blow would rather have been out there than stuck at his desk in the library cooking like pork. He had another four hours worth of thoughts like these. Not that being a library assistant was an uninteresting profession. It wasn't, it had its rewards on pretty much a daily basis. It was just that, on this particular day at least, it was too hot. That's all. Joe Blow wished it was winter.

Something else was niggling in the back of Joe Blow's mind too. He had been systematically snubbed. Well, not snubbed exactly. Nobody turned their nose up at Joe Blow. It was not even that he was ignored from time to time. No, it was much worse than that. That kind of snub was water off a duck's back to a man like Joe Blow. You see, if people chose to snub him, then at least he existed outside the realms of their own imagination. At least it was something palpable – a start. No, it wasn't that Joe Blow had been snubbed; it was the simple fact that he hadn't been noticed at all. This is what stuck in Joe Blow's mind like a fish bone in the throat. It happened everyday, since he first set foot in the place on his very first morning. Joe Blow was sure of that.

In fact, Joe Blow was seething. As the sun burst through the window it was the Head Librarian herself who was guilty as charged in his tired eyes. Joe Blow had worked in the library for five years – he started on the same day as two other colleagues. It was custom in the library for employees to be taken for lunch by the Head Librarian on a specific date in the fifth year of employment. Joe Blow had just been informed that his fellow "five year" colleagues had just set off to a restaurant in the centre of the town for a long lunch. Joe Blow had not even been invited despite his five year loyalty – and when he asked his immediate line manager about his omission from the library tradition he was given the following retort:

"Er, I'm sorry Joe, but it seems she didn't know who you were."

As you can imagine, Joe Blow was left ashen-faced. He walked back over to his untidy desk, incredulity welling inside. He just wanted the day to be over with; he just wanted to be outside, to find some fresh air, a breeze – to simply breathe different air. Joe Blow saw no real reason in protesting. What was the point in that? Nobody knew who he was anyway – or cared for that matter.

Joe Blow walked hurriedly down the steps from the library. The heat suffocated him. He gulped the air down into his lungs like a thirsty athlete sucking from a bottle of water. It felt good to be outside, but soon the humidity caught up with him causing his clothes to stick to his back and it weighed him down immediately; the very environment he existed within a heavy, burdensome Albatross around his sweaty neck. If there ever was a sword of Damocles then it was hanging directly above Joe

Blow there and then. And to be quite honest with you, he didn't care a jot if it was about to fall. He took his usual route across the playing fields towards the centre of the town.

It happened rather quickly really, as these things often seem to. Her scream shattered what ever vitriolic thoughts Joe Blow had. She was surrounded by three youths and one of them was holding a large knife to her throat. It glinted as it caught the sun. Joe Blow seemed to be the only other person in the vast field, the sole witness to the nefarious act before him. He looked around, the field was still deserted. He acted without thinking. He walked over to the three youths and the cowering woman. He immediately recognised her as a postgraduate from the library: a philosophy student to be precise. That very morning had he handed her John Gray's *Straw Dogs* over the counter. Joe Blow asked the question to the first youth who happened to look up.

"Excuse me, but could you tell me how to get to Albert Road, it's by the station apparently?"

And that was it, that's all he asked, that's all Joe Blow did. The rest, as they say, is history. The three youths, dumbfounded and perplexed by the upfront temerity of this question burst into paroxysms of juvenile laughter, before finally releasing the philosophy student and giving Joe Blow a "happy slap" while one youth filmed it on his mobile phone. The laughter echoed in Joe Blow's ringing ear as they ran away. The philosophy student immediately burst into tears of relief and gratitude.

The next week Joe Blow was in all the local and national newspapers – he even made it onto the local and national news. Everybody recognised him wherever he went. The story the tabloids couldn't get enough of was even picked up by *Richard & Judy* on Channel 4 and Joe Blow was scheduled to make a tea-time appearance on their TV show so Richard Madeley could ask the question everyone else had been asking him:

"So, Joe Blow, what made you think to ask these nasty little assailants directions to your very own street?"

The four minute interview with Richard & Judy went well. Joe Blow wasn't as monosyllabic as he first thought he was going to be. Although he found Richard Madeley a pedant, he quite liked Judy. In fact, he quite enjoyed his new found celebrity status. People, for once, actually began to ring him up, email him at work, buy him drinks; actually offer him seats on buses and taxi drivers gave him free rides. But most surprising of all the Head Librarian personally took him out for dinner at a top Italian restaurant in the centre of town – both as an apology for not treating him to his "five year" lunch and as a celebration of his heroic deed. Joe Blow spent the entire evening listening to elucidate her monotonous voice at how she felt he was such a "valued member of the library". Needless to say, Joe Blow hated his Head Librarian more than ever.

After one final magazine interview and a rather shambolic appearance on daytime TV show *Trisha* – in which Joe Blow was reunited with the philosophy student and, finding Trisha annoying at best, concluded that she reeked of too much expensive perfume – the interest in him began to slowly but surely thin out and soon his life slipped back in to the rhythm he was more accustomed to: the same repetitive malaise. Each tiresome day dissolving into the next as inertia finally took hold again. The summer came to an end.

One dark inclement day Joe Blow was sitting at his desk, minding his own business, he was extremely bored – so bored in fact he actually felt like walking out of the library there and then for good. He didn't of course, he just remained where he was supposed to, staring into his flat screen monitor, pretending to do some work. He was soon woken from his stupor by some commotion inside his office. There was a bonhomie wafting across the partitions that had not reared its head in a long time. A large group of Joe Blow's colleagues had gathered. Apparently it was the Arts & Humanities Librarian's birthday and the entire office was preparing to leave for the pub for a boozy lunch. This was the first Joe Blow had heard about it. He hurriedly picked up his rucksack and reached for his jacket. He looked up, was met with vacant, rather nonplussed stares, and before he could utter one syllable a new member of staff – who was considerably younger than him and had been at the library a mere four weeks – beat him to it:

"Okay, er, we're going for a tipple . . . Er . . . Er . . . Er . . . I'm sorry . . . What's your name?"

"My name's Joe Blow . . . Joe Blow . . . Joe . . . Blow . . ."

"Sorry Joe, we're just going out for a spot of lunch and a tipple for Jessica's Birthday . . ."

"Oh, I know, but don't worry about me, I'll stay here and man the . . ."

Before Joe Blow could finish they had walked out of the office. They took their guffaws and loud banter with them. Joe Blow sighed and stared at his flat screen monitor. He wished it was summer again.

Traffic Lights

"Well, what do you like then?"

"Me?"

"Yeah, you."

"Me, I like whippets."

"Whippets?"

"Yeah, whippets, much better than cats, are whippets."

"No they're not!"

"Yes they are."

"Why are whippets . . . Scrawny, shivering limp little whippets better than wise old cats, a species, may I say, that was worshipped as a deity in ancient Egypt, a species entwined in mythology throughout the ages . . . Why are whippets better than cats?"

"Easy, you can dress them up."

"What do you mean you can dress them up?"

"Well, you can put them in little coats and stuff, they love it, you can't do that with cats, they'd run a mile."

"Yeah, you're right, that's because a cat has dignity, you'd never catch a cat in a coat, and they're much cleverer than whippets."

"Oh yeah, and how do you work that one out?"

"Cats can climb trees, I mean, have you ever seen a whippet climb a tree?"

"No, no, I haven't, but why would a whippet need to climb a tree?"

"It's a life skill, one which they do not possess."

"But they can run, run like the wind, a cat can't."

"A cat doesn't need to run like the wind when it's a funambulist."

"A what?"

"A funambulist: a tightrope walker. Have you ever seen a cat step delicately atop a garden fence to escape the jaws of the neighbour's dog?"

"Yes, yes I have."

"Well, here ends the lesson, you see, whippets are not better than cats."

"Damn!"

"What?"

"We're on green, step on it or we'll be late for work, no time to be gabbling on about cats and dogs . . ."

'Innit'

Taylor Limehouse only had one month or so to go before he could officially leave school, but he did anyhow. He just walked out one lunchtime and didn't look back. His mother still thinks he attends school each day, but, to be honest, she wouldn't be that bothered if she found out he wasn't – she'd rather Taylor Limehouse was working and earning money for himself anyhow. He knew, she knew, and his teachers knew that he didn't stand much of a chance in his exams and that he wasn't going to attend – and even if he did he would probably just sit miserably twiddling his thumbs in the examination hall, doodling on the paper before him, one eye on the clock, the other on Sadie Young sitting in front of him.

Most days were spent with Pow Wow, or Phillip Greer as his mother knew him, playing on his X-Box and smoking weed. Pow Wow's mother smoked weed too, so everyone was happy, she didn't much care about what they were up to each day either. Pow Wow had recently told Taylor Limehouse about a crew he'd been hanging out with at night. They would roam

Upper Street in Islington after the clubs and bars had closed looking for lone drunken stragglers to steam, or mug, or attack. Whatever took their fancy. They, the crew, would film these muggings and random attacks on their mobile phones. Pow Wow said it was good fun and that Taylor Limehouse should join the crew, inviting him on their next outing. Pow Wow told Taylor Limehouse that it was good to do, that it was exciting and gave him a buzz, that it beats school and working, and that sometimes the unsuspecting victims' wallets are full of notes and cards. Taylor Limehouse told Pow Wow that he'd love to join the crew; he'd never been a member of a crew before and it felt like a good idea. Besides, Talor Limehouse didn't like the people who sat inside and outside the cafés and bars along Islington's Upper Street – the Essex Road was more his kind of place. The drinkers and revellers of Islington's trendy Upper Street all had different accents to him and sounded like his teachers, they wore big scarves and suit jackets and silly jeans that were far too skinny. The girls of Islington's Upper Street wouldn't look at him when he called out to them. Mostly he didn't like them because they were rich.

It was a Saturday night/Sunday morning, around 3.00 am. Islington's Upper Street was quite empty, except for random gaggles of revellers, homeless people, and street cleaners. Taylor Limehouse, Pow Wow, Richie, Dregz, and Razza were drinking Bacardi Breezers (stolen from an off licence on Essex Road earlier that evening), smoking, and waiting. Dregz had brought some skunk which they were busy enjoying. Taylor Limehouse wasn't nervous, he was excited, he was hoping that their future target was carrying a nice mobile phone, or even an iPod – he would have liked a new iPod.

They all sat along the curb by The Bull pub like a row of magpies on a branch waiting to take flight. Razza was playing some Grime on his mobile, nodding his head and throwing stones into the grid across the road. Dregz was bragging about the blow-job Tracey Gidley had given him the other night, laughing as he explained that his cum had gotten tangled in her hair and how she had had to walk home like that: "Like in dat film, man . . . Like in dat film, man" he kept on repeating, shaking with laughter. Taylor Limehouse had never had a blow-job before and was jealous – but he didn't say anything. He thought about what it would be like to get a blow-job from Sadie Young, he missed her now that he had left school – he didn't say that either.

Pow Wow pointed out the lone man. He was staggering across the road, past Sainsbury's, heading slowly towards Angel tube station. Razza smiled, nodded and put his mask on. Everyone stood up and masked-up too. They followed the lone man. Taylor Limehouse's heart was beginning to pump the blood faster and faster and faster. The crew walked in silence. Taylor Limehouse felt alive, he watched the lone man: he was in his late-twenties and looked like he was in one of those bands like Coldplay or Keane. Taylor Limehouse thought that he looked gay. Taylor Limehouse didn't like gays, and neither did the rest of his crew.

It all happened rather swiftly. Just as the lone man got to Islington Green by the entrance Richie switched on his mobile phone, it was like a signal, and immediately Pow Wow ran up to the lone man and hit him in the face as hard as he could. The lone man, due more to the shock of the blow than the power behind it, fell to the pavement. Dregz moved in and kicked him in the face as soon as he landed and then began to stamp on him. Richie simply laughed loudly as Taylor Limehouse delivered the first of his five punches. Soon the lone man was unconscious. Taylor Limehouse took his wallet and Dregz took his watch, Razza put out his spliff on his forehead, and Pow Wow just kicked him one last time for fun. The harsh contact of his Nike trainer on the lone man's head made a strange sound: it reminded Taylor Limehouse of his mother beating the mat from the kitchen on the doorstep in the back yard when she was cleaning the house.

"Did ya film it, did ya film it?" Pow Wow hollered at Richie as they ran away towards the Essex Road.

The crew divided up the thirty-one pounds between them. Dregz didn't tell the rest of his crew about the watch. He didn't much like it, but he was sure it was worth something. It had an engraving on the back, and Dregz read it over and over again:

" . . . for your 21st, with all our love, Mum and Dad. 2/3/2006"

[…]

The following week Taylor Limehouse was looking at his own face in the *Evening Standard.* And although the picture was taken from a CCTV camera and he was wearing a hood (recognisable to no one except those who knew him intimately and could see clearly that it was his hooded Nike top and Adidas tracksuit bottoms) his mother was still convinced the police would come knocking on their door any minute – even if the lone victim was now safely out of hospital. She was in tears. Pow Wow was sitting with them in the kitchen. He looked nonplussed. But Taylor Limehouse wasn't bothered. Taylor Limehouse was glowing. It was the first time his picture had appeared in a newspaper and he felt strange – he felt famous. He liked his picture being in the paper. He liked it a lot. He looked good too. The picture made him look taller and older. Bigger. If Sadie Young saw it she would recognise him immediately and want to be with him. Taylor Limehouse turned to his mother.

"What ya cryin for? No one's gonna come knockin' . . . No one knows dat's me . . . Am flyin' me, da world's ma oyster, innit?"

Taylor Limehouse's mother got up from the kitchen table, lit a cigarette, and walked out of the room. Taylor Limehouse bagan to laugh.

The Doppelgänger

(Although I never thought it possible). When the myriad tentacle-like slippery arms of Her Majesty's Government finally tracked me down and requested my imminent presence for Jury Service it made me ecstatically happy. Not that law or the British Justice system interested me that much, but simply because it gave me at least two weeks respite from the intolerable cretins who populated my place of work.

(For this particular story, like others you may have read, neither my name nor my place of work is important. You've seen it all before. No, what's important here is that I had found, through no fault of my own, an escape route, albeit an ephemeral one, and I was willing to dive head first into it.)

When I told a friend, a graphic designer originally from Belfast, she informed me:

"Where I come from you may have well have signed your own death sentence when agreeing to be a juror . . ."

(I didn't care.) Sometimes I'd rather be dead anyway than have to go to work each day – that was a death sentence in itself. No, I was happy to walk into my local Crown Court on that cold, bitter morning. I remember sitting with the other jurors in the waiting room, which wasn't too dissimilar to a GP's waiting room on any local high street. Most of the jurors, about fifty in total, looked quite happy to be there too. Some read books or newspapers, some knitted, most chatted amongst themselves in little hierarchical groups, the loudest being those already sworn in as jurors and currently sitting in on a trial. Some looked like seasoned professionals, almost like they'd spent their entire lives doing this public duty. Others seemed to be gloating, rather superciliously one might add, delirious that they had been picked – blatantly disregarding the sheer randomness of the court's crude lottery system used to pick each juror.

I remember opening my book and finding the room far too stuffy, shifting in my seat far more than usual, having to reread paragraphs because I'd inadvertently skimmed over them. I soon became quite bored and put my book to one side, sighing momentarily, the novelty disappearing far quicker than

I ever thought it would. I looked about the room, picking out interesting faces, trying to guess what it was they did for a living, what, if any, secrets they were hiding, trying to dig out from them any secret misery.

And then I saw him. He was definitely my size and bulk, the same light brown complexion. He was dressed almost identically to me too, which I found most odd. The same sartorial idiosyncrasies: cheap black jacket with bucket pockets, scarf, that sort of thing. He had on a good pair of black leather shoes, as I did. The more I looked at him, the more I noticed the same features on his face: the sharp long nose, the hollow cheeks, the brown eyes, the faint eyebrows, the thick lips, the crooked front teeth. (I shuddered; he must be my doppelgänger. Just like in the book.) I looked about the room, no one had noticed us; no one had noticed the uncanny resemblance. (Surely they must have noticed something? Even on that odd subconscious level people seem to talk about? I mean, what are the chances of such a thing? How utterly odd. Why, for a start, doesn't he look up? Why hasn't he noticed me? Why hasn't he sensed my presence as I have his? Why, damn him, doesn't he look my way?)

I remember, now, these questions quite clearly. Thoughts cascaded into me like fresh cold water from a tap. (Should I walk over to him and introduce myself? Make polite chit-chat with him? Walk by him from time to time in the vain hope that he'll notice me?) To be quite honest I didn't quite know what to do. It really was quite unnerving though, having him there in the very same room. We looked exactly alike – even his hair had the same kink in the back, the same wave above the left ear. It was even the same colour, which in itself is quite an extraordinary feat, as my hair was once described by a hairdresser as "being unlike any shade, tint or hue" he had ever seen in his twenty-seven year career. I soon began to sweat, I needed to speak to him; he was me. I was looking at myself.

Suddenly an old grey-haired lady, probably retired, sat herself beside me. I looked at her and smiled. She leant in closer to me.

"I've just been speaking to your twin. Strange that isn't it?"

"What?"

"Twins both called for Jury Service in the same week?"

"Pardon?"

"Twins . . ."

I immediately looked over to him, me, my doppelgänger. He had gone, he wasn't there. I looked around the room, feeling quite dizzy and peculiar. I turned back to the old grey-haired lady.

"What did he say to you? Where has he gone?"
"Oh, happen he's been picked for a case. He was just sitting over there. I was speaking with him earlier in the canteen, whilst we were queuing for earl grey tea. I like earl grey . . ."
"What did he say? What did he say?"
"He just mentioned that he hoped he got picked as soon as possible, as he was quite bored, said that he had better things to do at work, that he was a busy man, quite important . . ."
"Where is he now?"
"He must've got himself picked . . ."

I turned to stare at my shoes; I tapped my right foot; I thought about my twin. It was absurd. They'd picked him. (Why not me?

What does he have that I haven't?) It's not that we looked any different. It couldn't be that one looked more trustworthy than the other. I soon stopped myself, my thoughts were spiralling out of control, and besides, the system was a lottery and nothing to do with the way I looked. It didn't make me feel much better though. We were soon told that we could go for lunch; we had an hour to entertain ourselves at Her Majesty's pleasure. I had a dreadful chicken curry; well, that's what I thought it was meant to be. Just as I was about to get up from my seat I saw him. Once again he was sitting on the other side of the room from me; once again he hadn't noticed me. I didn't know what to do. My heart was pounding and it felt like the blood coursing through my body was being pushed to its limits. I decided that I should talk to him, or at least try to gain his attention.

I slowly rose to my feet and began to walk over to him; I clutched my belongings tightly to my chest as if carrying an injured or sleeping child, and then another strange thing happened: his mobile phone began to ring and he answered it, and the name he used was my name. (It was my name!) I stood there, frozen, and glared at him. Not once did he look up. Not once did he notice me standing there, my glare burning into him. I began to feel a little nauseous. He seemed pleased to be speaking to whoever it was on the other end of the line. My mind began to race away from me again. I wanted to know who it was he was talking to. Just why he was using my name. I turned and walked out of the canteen and stood behind the door; I had to think hard about this. The minutes began to tick by on the large clock above the exit, I watched the seconds eke across its face. I was shaking. I walked back into the canteen and over to him – me – without blinking.

"Excuse me . . ."

"Yes."

"What's your name?"

"My name is ______ why?"

"But that's *my* name!"

"It's a small world isn't it?"

"But don't you think that's odd?"

"Not really."

"But we even look the same! The same size, the same face, the same colour hair, colour eyes . . . We're even wearing the same shoes, clothes . . ."

"Pure coincidence, nothing extraordinary . . ."

"But, but you're my doppelgänger, my twin, you even sound like me!"

"Yes, it happens."

"How can you be so . . . So . . . So fucking nonchalant about this?"

"Bigger things happen . . ."

"What do you mean, bigger things can happen?"

"Well, take the case I'm on . . . A murder. Wouldn't you say a murder is bigger, in every conceivable way, than a mere fluke, a coincidence?"

"They're two completely different things . . ."

"Maybe, and one is bigger than the other."

"Okay, but will you at least admit the fact that you are me and I am you is just a tad phantasmagorical?"

"No. I look like many people. As, no doubt, you and many other people do."

"What do you mean you look like many people?"

"You're not the only person I look like . . ."

"What do you mean?"

"Think about it."

I got up and immediately walked away, fearing that he was most probably mad, a court interloper of some sort. I needed to alert the authorities of his presence. Maybe he was a risk, especially to me. I left the canteen feeling rather cold, shivering like I'd seen a ghost – not that I believed in such rubbish. A strange fear suddenly gripped me that slowly turned into a mild rage.

(Surely he was as amazed as I was at the fact that we were identical in every conceivable way? What was wrong with the man? Surely he could see that this wasn't some everyday coincidence? Surely he could see how sinister all this was? I mean, it's not every day you stumble upon your doppelgänger – especially one with the same name. Surely this is the stuff of fiction? A creative act committed to celluloid?)

I walked towards the first Court Usher I saw – she was a peroxide blonde, a hard-faced Cockney-type.

"Have you seen the man?"

"The man?"

"The man in the canteen who looks like me, exactly like me?"

Er . . . No . . . I haven't, sir. Why?"

"Because he shouldn't be here, there's something wrong with him . . ."

"What do you mean?"

"Has he just walked in off the street?"

"Isn't he a juror?"

"He's not right, he's got a screw loose, he's got my name . . ."

"Oh, really, and what's your name?"

"My name, his name, is ______."

"Okay then ______, show me where he is."

I took the Court Usher back to the canteen. I opened the door. He was sitting just where I had left him moments earlier. I pointed over to him. He was reading a book, I looked a little closer. He was reading Iain Sinclair's *Dining On Stones, Or The Middle Ground.* I laughed. Of course. It had to be. It was the very same book I was reading. (Him!). The Court Usher walked over to my doppelgänger. I followed her. She loomed over him. He immediately looked up from his – my – book. First at her, and then at me. He smiled.

"Hullo again . . ."

"This man, here, thinks you're an intruder, do you have any form of identification, your summons?"

"Why, of course I do . . . My name's ______, and here is my summons . . . And, I'm a juror in Courtroom 6 . . ."

The Court Usher glanced at his details and then turned to me.

"Your interloper seems to be who he says he is . . ."

"But, but . . ."

I didn't really know what to say. I remember not being able to form any words, my mouth just hanging open.

"Okay then, I'll be seeing you both."

The Court Usher walked away and left us both together again at the table. I stared at my feet, feeling most peculiar, and then turned to head for the nearest exit. I was sick of my public duty. I wanted out. I'd rather have been sitting at my desk at work with the bozos than in that canteen with him, me. Just as I began to walk away he called out my name.

"How do you know my name?"

"You told me it was the same as mine . . . Now that you're here you may as well stay for a coffee . . ."

I stopped dead in my tracks and slowly turned to face him – face me – because that's how it looked to me anyway.

"Well, I'd prefer something stronger . . . But . . ."

"Have your coffee black then . . ."

By now the canteen was quite empty, not even the sullen-looking kitchen staff seemed to be present. A heavy stench of overcooked cheap-beef stew, chicken curry, vegetarian whatnots dripping in cheese fat, black coffee and rock-hard flapjacks wafted over. Cheap canteen smells. I couldn't look at him – me – let alone instigate some type of conversation. He continued to smile, gesturing over to the coffee pot in the corner of the room. I simply nodded. He got up from the table and walked slowly over to the coffee-pot. I couldn't even stop him to give him my daily allowance card. He walked back over to the table with two mugs of coffee, both black. He sat himself back in the same chair opposite me. I sat myself down. He had stopped smiling.

"You and I aren't the same person, you know . . ."

"No?"

"No."

"Oh."

"We're miles apart . . . Great chasms separate us."

"Why's that?"

"Because we look at life differently, we couldn't be more diametrically opposed to each other if we tried, even if we look alike, share the same name, read the same books . . . All that is superfluous to the core reason we are here . . ."

"What do you mean?"

"I mean, for example . . . Existence."

"And?"

"Well, for you it's an escape, just like this public duty is for you."

"And?"

"For me it's a hindrance . . ."

"Oh, why . . . ?"

"Because I could be working, I could be contributing for real . . . The hanging weight of existence looming above like a guillotine would be a mere shadow if I was busying myself with work."

"And?"

"You, you just see things as a giant playground, governed by your own making, where you can shirk . . . Put simply, you are nothing but a waster with dreams."

"And what are you?"

"I am my own man, of course . . ."

"But, you're clearly a slave, a slave to work."

"No I'm not. Work is pleasure. I am work."

"Preposterous!"

"Why so?"

"Because it's a ball and chain, that's why. We are unable to breathe whilst shackled by its influence."

"Ha! Work gives life!"

"Work destroys mine!"

"Work is joy!"

"Work is agony!"

"Work is deliverance!"

"Work is penance!"

The conversation continued like this until he – me – began to get angry.

"You're a waste of space!"

"Oh, and why's that?"

"You will never be able to contribute to anything society offers."

"What, and you will?"

"Why, of course. Tell me, why do you think you haven't been picked yet?"

"Eh?"

"You're not one of us, that's why. People can see straight through you. You are as transparent as the air we breathe."

"What have I done?"

"You didn't engage. You hid in the corner. You didn't realise your full potential."

"I don't want to . . . Not in an environment of work and orders."

"What about *money*?"

"What *about* money?"

"Does it not appeal to you?"

"Not really?"

"Why?"

"Because why should it? I can live the life I lead with the money I've got."

"Don't you want more?"

"No."

"Then you're a fucking imbecile! Work!"

"I would prefer not to . . ."

With this he glared at me. To say that I was incredulous was a bit of an understatement. I wanted to rip his – my? – throat out. I mean, how dare he just waltz into my life and pick at my bones like a dog.

(How could a man, who was basically me, who looked just like me, shared the same name, read the same literature, how could a man who was ultimately me be so fucking different? How could he act the way he did? Work this! Work that! What's he talking about? How can a man speak this way? Doesn't he understand that there is a different way to look at this horrid span we so fleetingly possess? Doesn't he realise that we simply don't have to work? We live in a humdrum society governed by men like him. They are everywhere, there is no escaping them. Wherever you turn there they are! Wherever you run to there they are! Stalking you! The henchmen of doom, that's who they are. Omnipotent monsters. Nothing more, nothing less.)

Again I walked away, but this time I didn't look back. I left him – me – there, in the canteen. I walked out of the building and onto the busy street. I watched the cars, lorries, vans and cyclists pass me by. I took a deep breath. I had quite a few choices, there were many things I could have done. I did none of them. I walked into the nearest public house.

I had exactly twenty-three minutes before I had to be officially back inside the jurors' waiting room. I ordered a pint of Guinness. I was surrounded by business types of all ages in sharp, expensive suits, happy and content business types drinking warm bitter in the couple of hours they had been allocated. The very same hours they are allocated each and every day. It wasn't for me. It never would be.

The Overdraft

"Ah, finally . . ."

"Good morning, David speaking, how may I help you? . . ."

"Well, I need an, I need you to extend my overdraft, if you will."

"Okay, could I have your account number please?"

"Yes, it's, oh, wait a minute I can never quite remember the damn thing. Here we go, yes, I have my cheque book at hand. Okay . . . 100783409 . . . Okay?"

"Good morning Mr Little . . . Could I just ask you a couple of security questions?"

"Yeah . . ."

"Can you give me your date of birth?"

"02/04/73 . . ."

"And can you give me your mother's maiden name?"

"Hill . . ."

"Okay, how can I help you Mr Little?"

"Well, I, well I just explained why . . ."

"Okay, and what was that?"

"Well, I need an extension to my overdraft . . ."

"Okay . . ."

"Yeah, I need to extend it to about £2500 . . ."

"Okay . . ."

"Yeah, I need an . . ."

"Can you just hold on one moment? I just need to refer this to a colleague, um, okay . . .?"

"Um, yeah, okay."

". . ."

"Hullo . . ."

". . ."

"Hullo . . ."

"Mr Little . . ."

"Yes?"

"No, I'm afraid we can't allow that."

"Why not?"

"Well, because no money has entered your account for the last four months. You don't have enough to cover any future repayments . . ."

"Oh, I know, but I've started a new job, I get paid at the end of the month . . ."

"Okay, but, we just can't allow that kind of loan."

"But I need to, I need to pay my rent, buy food, dare I say it . . . Socialise."

"I can understand that Mr Little, it's just that no money has entered . . ."

"But I just told you I've started a new job, I don't get paid until the end of the month . . ."

"It's just not possible, Mr Little . . ."

"But I need a break, I need to pay my rent, I need your help, just this once . . ."

"I'm afraid that . . ."

"But come on . . . Surely you can understand . . ."

"Understand what Mr Little . . . ?"

"The fact that I'm on my arse, that I need help . . ."

"But we can't help. We can't loan you the money. I understand."

"But I've just started, I get paid at the end of the month, I write as well, short stories, novels, I've just sent my novel to a publisher . . . I'm not some scrounger . . ."

"Yes, but . . ."

"Yes but what?"

"Yes, but . . ."

“Yes but do you actually know how hard one has to work at completing a novel? Do you know how much effort it takes? Do you know how it takes over your entire existence? The hours, the loneliness, the dedication . . .”

“But, Mr Little, no money has . . .”

“How can I dedicate my time every day towards something I don’t believe in? Like some lousy office drone? How can I when the novel just consumes me? 95,000 words my novel, my work, do you know how much time that takes? Do you know how much time and devotion that takes?”

“Well . . . Yes, I do . . .”

“Eh?”

“Well, yes I do as a matter of fact . . .”

“Oh, you do, how?”

“Well, I’m writing a novel too, Mr Little . . .”

“Yeah, right.”

“I am Mr Little . . . I’m sending my first five chapters to my agent today . . . I’m a writer like you . . .”

“Your agent? . . . Bollocks! . . . You work in a bank for fuck’s sake . . . You don’t have time to write . . .”

“I do, Mr Little . . .”

"When? In between meetings? . . ."

"No, at night. I don't socialise you see . . . I just write."

"Rubbish . . . Give me an overdraft, you lackey!"

"Mr Little, as I've already explained to you, it's just not possible . . . And believe me, I do sympathise with you, I really do . . . It's just that . . ."

"Yeah, as you said, you write too . . . Goodbye, you fucking slave . . ."

"Goodbye Mr Little . . . Sorry we couldn't . . ."

"Yeah."

". . ."

The Conversation

It was two weeks before payday and all he had left of his national just-above-average wage was enough to purchase himself a bottle of Magner's Irish cider. It was a Thursday afternoon. The Artillery, Bunhill Fields. He walked up to the bar without hesitation – as if his pockets were overspilling with dosh. An act of defiance. The transaction was soon completed. The cold cider tasted good even though it attacked his teeth. He sat down on the nearest table and picked up a discarded *NME* somebody had left behind. He read solidly for ten minutes or so about bands and individuals he neither knew nor cared about before the two figures sat themselves down beside him at the next table. He didn't look at them because he had noticed something floating in his cider – it looked like cigarette ash, or grit from someone's shoe, or – heaven forbid – from under the grotty barmaid's fingernails. He stared at his unnaturally orange drink before him. He couldn't touch it, let alone drink it, nor could he walk over to the grotty barmaid and change it. Such behaviour would be far too embarrassing for him, especially now he was undoubtedly penniless. He listened to the conversation of the two men beside him. It was hushed, secretive – obviously they had been friends for a long time, just by their natural demeanour he could tell this. Either that or they were lovers, but he found this conclusion highly improbable as, although, their conversation was hushed and secretive, it wasn't intimate, it wasn't coded in any way – especially in that way.

Whatever it was they were talking about they certainly didn't want anyone else to hear. This was the only real conclusion that made any sense to him. So he continued to listen to them, struggling to find context, a picture, a choice word here or there that could help him find their track.

He hated his life, of course. He hated the fact that he only had enough money for one drink no matter where he was. There was nothing more in his life; nothing less either: it was a perpetual motion of nothingness, a mere blip on a scale of zero to ad infinitum. Endless possibilities he couldn't afford. Endless possibilities he just couldn't grasp. So he relented and relished his one drink with abandon – he didn't have anything else.

So, he listened to the two strangers beside him because they had something, a shared belief, something between them that didn't belong to anyone else. He listened to them because, put simply, they weren't him.

They, the two strangers, huddled close: one smoking, the other intermittently biting his nails. He leant in to listen but couldn't pick up one single syllable, let alone a word or sentence. It was impossible to hear them over the dreadful music, the chattering of the other punters, the barmaid's cackle, the traffic on the road outside. They could only hear each other – just they way they liked it.

Soon he began to get quite annoyed. His drink was good though now, and however much he tried to make it last he couldn't. He wanted more, as always. But apart from this horrible void in his life he just wanted to know what they were talking about, that's all. Even if it was meaningless drivel, he didn't care; he just wanted to know what the fuck it was they wanted to keep from everyone else.

He finished his drink. He waited, hanging on to each sound their huddled form produced, but still he couldn't work out just what was keeping them locked in that secretive huddle. He knew that if he had been drunk he would have asked them. He'd have walked up to them, sat down at their table and introduced himself like it was the most natural thing in the world. That's what he would've done if he could have just afforded one more drink. He thought about them buying him drinks, accepting him into their fold, the three of them huddled together in secret confabulation.

Soon two men, one considerably fatter than the other, sat themselves down at the other table next to the secretive huddle. They turned and stared at the two men talking; it was obvious that they could hear every word. They began to talk to each other, about what they could hear – the newcomers made sure that everyone could hear them.

"What are they doing in here anyway? I thought their sort didn't drink?"

"Looks like they're up to no fucking good to me."

“Probably planning another bombing.”

“Or a chemical fucking attack.”

The two men in the secretive huddle quickly finished their drinks and left. As they were passing his table he heard one of them whisper:

“I’m more scared of being beaten up by skinheads than a terrorist bomb . . .”

The pub was now enveloped in a volley of racist banter as the two men chatted to themselves making sure that everyone could hear them, happy that the secretive huddle had been disbanded. He couldn’t get back to work quickly enough.

The Roof

It was two o'clock in the afternoon on what had been announced as the hottest day of the year so far. Irvine Doyle had been sitting at his desk, staring into his snazzy new flat-screen monitor since eight o'clock that very same morning. Apart from, that is, the hours of eleven and twelve when he counted the pigeons that glided past his window and the multitudinous rooftops of London. He counted four hundred and forty three give or take a couple, although he realised he could have been counting the same group over and over again. This didn't concern him. Irvine Doyle quite liked pigeons.

He was now alone. His colleagues were at the pub, he had been asked to go but had politely declined the offer – much to the perplexity of his fellow colleagues. Irvine Doyle didn't usually turn down such invitations. Anything would usually suffice to get him out of the office for a while. But this particular day was quite different, a thick cloud of inertia had suddenly descended from the ether, it cloaked Irvine Doyle with indifference. He simply didn't care what he did, or what was happening. Such feelings had never manifested themselves in such a manner before. Irvine Doyle didn't quite understand what was happening to him.

The office was quiet; only the perpetual mechanical drone of the air-conditioning unit reverberated throughout the building (imagine a gleaming structure that seemed, at first glance at least, to be made solely from glass). Irvine Doyle momentarily looked away from his snazzy flat-screen monitor and turned to look out of his window, peering down across the company courtyard to the building opposite (imagine a red brick uniformed affair, erected circa 1930 most probably when office blocks of this type looked modern and clean in design and didn't serve as a huge blank canvas for Banksy-like graffiti on every conceivable façade). This building across the company courtyard, which Irvine Doyle looked at most days, was now occupied by squatters. Most days he would look over to the new, arty, occupants gathering for tea, exercise or whatever it was he thought they were doing on the roof.

That roof, how Irvine Doyle wanted to be on that roof on that particular day; just sitting, drinking wine, smoking whatever it was they smoked, bathing under the sun, reading a book, enjoying his own time whilst looking over to the office workers in the towering, modern, glass affair across the spotless courtyard and grinning to himself, safe in the knowledge that he didn't have to spend his days chained to his miserable desk. This small, personal thought that belonged solely to Irvine Doyle was bliss, utter untouchable bliss.

Irvine Doyle would turn away and close his ears when his colleagues, who sat around him, uttered their dissent.

"Why don't they just get jobs?"
"Why don't they pay their taxes like everyone else?"
"Why don't they earn their own money instead of spending their parents'?"
"Why don't they contribute to society?"

Irvine Doyle would turn away, he'd ignore the glib comments and nod his head, feigning acquiescence when he thought appropriate, wishing quite secretly that he was on that roof instead of there, by his miserable desk, trying not to listen to his colleagues' protestations.

He looked back over to his snazzy flat-screen monitor, he had thirty-two unopened emails to read – all of them work related. He switched off his PC. He looked back over to the roof. At first he thought it was just a man sawing wood on a work bench or something, but then he noticed that the young, rather muscular, man was naked. Then he noticed, little by little, the wondrous naked woman in front of the muscular young man, kneeling, and her round, shapely, heart-shaped arse there for all to see, the muscular man furiously pumping his prick into her, rhythmically without a care in the world. Never had Irvine Doyle seen such disregard, such open unashamed freedom, such dazzling vanity. It was sex, a coming together, not just for the two participants, but for all. It was a defiant slap in the face to each and every office worker peering down upon them, a primal scream announcing to all that there was another way, that you didn't have to follow the herd, that you could stand out from the rest, that you could shine, no matter how absurd you looked.

Irvine Doyle continued to look down, across the roof, over the company courtyard towards the hypnotic spectacle of the muscular young man and the brazen woman fucking like crazy for all to see. It was the greatest thing he had ever witnessed. It was magnificent. It was defiant. Even the pigeons had stopped to have a look. He counted fifty-four in total. The copulating couple continued their heavenly pursuit regardless.

He immediately walked over to the looming window, he watched their every move, and it was a peculiar pornography, somewhat more tangible than he was used to. It was as if he could feel their pleasure, their release, their shocking abandon, their base indifference to the mechanisms around them: the city and its manipulated occupants governed by its tentacle-like reasoning, tickling, persuading, forcing each decision, each business meeting, each deal and it was theirs alone – and it always would be – and for that golden sun-drenched moment on that rooftop they knew it. And Irvine Doyle knew it. And everyone else who had caught a sneaky peek knew it too. He thought them more than magnificent; he thought them ethereal, superhuman even. He felt beneath them and it was like they knew something about existence he never could, so he continued to watch them, mesmerised by their outlandish brilliance, wishing it was him, wishing he was there and not where he was. Wishing he understood life enough not to care about it.

Soon the dazzling copulation finished, both the muscular young man and the compliant woman stretched and looked over to Irvine Doyle's office – it was as if they knew he was there, all alone, watching them. It was as if they had put on the whole show especially for him, in order to prove a point that had been staring him in the face for a long time, a point he'd been waiting for all his working life.

He watched as they put their discarded clothes back on: a t-shirt here, a thong there. Soon they rolled and lit up a giant spliff, each inhaling the dark blue smoke into their awaiting lungs.

Soon Irvine Doyle's colleagues returned from their boozy lunch, chattering and laughing. He watched as they dumped their coats and bags by their desks before rattling their computers to check their emails on their equally as snazzy flat-screen monitors. At that moment he decided not to inform his colleagues about the live performance that had happened just a few moments ago below them on the roof across from the company courtyard, instead he decided to compose a letter of resignation and deliver it to his immediate Line Manager that very afternoon. And, inwardly, he would dedicate that eloquently written letter to the muscular young man and the shapely woman on the roof and he would tell no one about that either, as Irvine Doyle knew that in moments such as he now found himself, unlike the muscular young man and the beautiful woman on the roof, it was much better to keep things to himself.

Dead End

Samuel Grady had only been dead two days. His body was lying in some exhaust fume-stained funeral parlour off Liverpool Road in north London. Nobody was really bothered, or aware for that matter. So there he remained – for the time being anyhow – stiff, decaying, dead meat.

[…]

Meanwhile, in Southwark, south of the murky Thames, Thomas Grady, his younger brother, was delicately caressing the left cheek of a young girl he'd only just met two hours before this most intimate of encounters, oblivious to his brother's death. Her skin was soft to the touch, pinkish in hue; she had big hazel eyes. Thomas Grady looked into them.

"You know, I feel we were destined to meet . . ."

"Do you?"

"Yes, I do . . . I mean . . ."

"Why?"

"Why what?"

"Why do you think we were destined to meet?"

"I don't know, we just were, I guess . . ."

"Maybe . . ."

"Yeah, maybe . . ."

It wasn't destiny that had brought them together; they had met by chance; at Bankside, the Thames lapping below – it was high-tide. Both were there to find that house – the one some recent book was about. It had been reviewed in all the broadsheets that week. Boredom rather than curiosity had brought them together. Both Thomas Grady and the young woman with the soft, pinkish cheeks and big hazel eyes were ever-so-disappointed with the house. Both immediately recognised this disappointment in each other, both could sense each other's perplexity. So they went for a drink in a little pub near Bear Street. Thomas Grady continued to caress her soft pinkish cheek. She blinked a couple of times and tilted her head.

[...]

Samuel Grady's naked, emaciated body was pulled out and placed with authority on to the cold stainless steel table. First his pale emaciated body was sprayed with disinfectant and cleansed with a crude germicidal soap by hand. Next a small incision was made below the neck to allow access to a major artery. The bored parlour assistant then inserted a tube through which an arterial chemical was flushed into Samuel Grady's body, cleansing each artery, vein and cell while the thickening, gloopy-like blood was sucked out from his limp form via a prominent vein in his milk-bottle leg. His stomach, still possessing an undigested meal, swelled up just a little as the fluid coursed through his dead veins; his wretched body prodded here and there from time to time by the assistant. Soon his veins were drained of blood. He was ready for a cavity inspection. The release of liquids or gasses, that had built up after his death, in the abdominal and chest cavities needed to be thoroughly removed. Another incision was made into Samuel Grady's pathetic torso, this time in the abdomen. Yet more tubes were stuffed into him, and the noxious gasses and putrid liquids were, once again, forcibly sucked out until not one drop of scum was left behind. Soon, after certain organs had been removed, and when the skin had begun to dry out, he would be touched up with unsophisticated make-up – naturally he would be made to look like he had blood running through him again, with a dab of rouge here and some concealer there; his eyes glued tight with a strong epoxy resin in the hope that he would look like he was sleeping in peace. Finally, with the rudimentary procedure over, he would be finally left to rot before either the flames or the worms could get to him.

[…]

Thomas Grady's next thought was how to get this young woman into bed. Or, at least, somewhere a little more private, where he could achieve more than the fleeting caress of her soft, pinkish cheek.

"So, do you fancy going . . . ?"

"Back to your place?"

"Well, er, yes . . . Back to my place . . ."

"Well, I'd much prefer it if we went back to my place, I don't live that far from here, you see, and I would much prefer it if we did this in my own surroundings . . ."

[…]

Samuel Grady's body was drained and hollowed. His innards removed and placed into a black bag. His heart, liver and lungs lay beside him – Samuel Grady not being a cadaver as such, but conscientious enough in life. The mortician and his assistant moved around his body with precision and routine – a ritual acted out a thousand times before. Their thoughts were elsewhere of course and there were other things they could have been doing, it being a Saturday afternoon, but they had mortgages to pay, families to feed; it was fast approaching Christmas and gadgets and other technological must-haves needed to be acquired. Such things cost dearly. The weekend overtime was money well-earned. And well-spent hopefully. Other than Samuel Grady there were six other bodies to prepare before five o'clock. Lunch would, as always, have to be taken on the job. The stench of congealed blood didn't bother them in the slightest. Years of such practice had rendered each immune to such grim mementos of their frail mortality. The assistant chomped on a roast beef and horseradish brown granary roll, while the mortician ate a day old, cold, fish-finger and tomato ketchup on thick, home-made white bread. They ate in silence, using the cold stainless steel table that Samuel Grady was placed on, to rest their weary elbows – occasionally the assistant would pick out the crumbs that had fallen into Samuel Grady's deep, hairy belly-button. The other prickly black hairs gathered on his arms, chest, thighs, back and between his legs not bothering them in the slightest. Munch. Munch. Munch.

Samuel Grady's eyes were fixed shut, not that their lunching on the job and complete disrespect would have bothered him anyway. He was fully aware that this awkward moment was always on the cards – it was just a shame that he wasn't around to witness it. The mortician and his assistant finished their sandwiches.

[…]

They walked into her flat; six floors toward the bruised London skyline. The Tate Modern could be seen from each of the many windows – as could the Thames. The young woman with the soft pinkish cheeks and the big hazel eyes began to make coffee. Thomas Grady sank into a comfortable armchair, watching her every move across the open-plan room. The coffee aroma filled the air, occupying the atmosphere like a spectre. Thomas Grady noticed the curvature of her arse as she bent over to find a tray from a cupboard. Eventually she walked back over to him carrying the cafetiere, white espresso cups and warm frothy milk on a red tray. Thomas Grady didn't touch his coffee; he immediately started to caress her thigh. It felt soft and extremely supple. She began to sigh.

The sexual intercourse that was to follow this clumsy move didn't last that long, but it was intense and probably the best sex each of them had pretty much experienced. Thomas Grady looked into those big hazel eyes.

"Do you think we should see each other again?"
"I don't know . . ."
"Why?"
"Well, it's not everyday I take men back to my flat for sex."

"But it was good."

"Yes . . . It was . . ."

"Yes."

"Yes."

". . ."

". . ."

"Okay."

"Okay, what?"

"We should see each other again."

"When?"

"Next week."

"Okay, next week."

"Can I have your number?"

"Yes."

[…]

Samuel Grady's body was catalogued along with the others. All the relevant paperwork was filled out by the assistant. This information was then entered onto a PC. Each file was then saved onto disc. Photocopies were also made of each printed hard-copy; invoices and forms filed. Everything was meticulously put in its place. The routine was executed with precision and Samuel Grady's stiff, hollow body was finally covered to the shoulders and stored with the others.

[...]

The following week, after his brother's quite sombre funeral, Thomas Grady met the young woman with the soft pinkish cheeks and big hazel eyes. This time they went out for a drink north of the river in a small pub near Old Street, quite close to where Thomas Grady lived. This time the sex was pretty bad. After it had ended, back at his small flat without a view, they lay next to each other in silence. Thomas Grady was trying to work out why it had been so sterile, while she, on the other hand, was trying to work out an excuse to leave.

"You know, I'd better be going . . ."

"Yes?"

"Yes."

"Right."

"Yeah, I have to visit a friend in Wimbledon, it's quite far . . ."

"Yes, it is . . ."

"Yes."

"So . . ."

"So . . ."

"Yes, I'll better be off . . ."

"Yes."

"Good-bye."

"Good-bye."

She dressed quickly, not even giving Thomas Grady much time to look at her body one last time and before he could get up to open the door for her she was out into the corridor. He immediately lit up a cigarette and began to think about his brother; they'd not seen that much of each other in recent years and the funeral had passed him by. Thomas Grady started to cry – he missed him.

[…]

Samuel Grady was buried next to his mother and father in a

Catholic cemetery in north London. The rain, it seemed, lashed down on the disturbed earth the whole week after his burial. It was rather black and silent down there.

Being Lee Rourke Is Boring

At 3.00 pm on most Sunday afternoons Lee Rourke can be found sitting at the bar of The French House in Soho. He first heard about this idiosyncratic little public house over ten years ago when somebody or other informed him it was the boozer where Dylan Thomas had lost his manuscript of *Under Milk Wood* down the back of a bench after a rather turbulent evening, only for it to be found the next morning by Gaston, the old landlord at the time. Lee Rourke rather liked this tale, not because it was of a literary persuasion, although it helped, but because it signified to him that such a boozer welcomed and, in fact, encouraged raucous drinking – it being, after all, a public house. It seemed to be, to Lee Rourke at least, a boozer that took care of its drunks.

Lee Rourke ordered his first drink in The French House the following weekend where he was smugly told by the well-spoken barman (who has since disappeared):

"We haven't sold pints in here since 1949 . . . Halves only, sir!"

Each Sunday afternoon Lee Rourke likes to sit by the window on a stool drinking good red or white and taking liberal advantage of the free bowls of mixed marinated olives while reading a book, writing in his Moleskine, or looking out onto Soho's busy Dean Street if the window is open. Then, settled, he waits patiently for the conversations to begin. The "conversations" are the regulars, whose portraits adorn the walls like black and white spectres, reminding newcomers that they already exist, that they are valued, that they are interesting, successful and talented. That they are not, in fact, you. In real life they all have ruddy faces and stink of expensive perfume and cigar smoke; they stand at the bar and speak with loud cynical, plummy accents. Some are American who sponge off their parents' past glories, others are burnt-out actors and theatre types, there are even a few coke-addled old ex-*Coronation Street* regulars. Many are writers, bibliophiles, academics, conmen, aristocrats, commoners, Cockneys, transvestites, pimps, rent-boys, and queens. All are alcoholics to greater or lesser degrees.

Lee Rourke likes to sit and watch them, listening to the myriad subjects their boozy conversations generate, observing their exaggerated mannerisms and hackneyed gesticulations. They never speak to Lee Rourke. They don't even notice he's there. He's not one of them. Lee Rourke is not lonely though. He doesn't envy them in the slightest. He finds them amusing. In fact, Lee Rourke rather likes them.

[...]

It was a Sunday like any other Sunday. As regular as an atomic clock, at 4.23 pm to be precise, the two artists entered The French House. One of the artists was considerably taller than the other. Lee Rourke put down the book he was reading. The artists' clothes were expensive and black – probably Prada. The taller artist was wearing a red Tootal scarf. Lee Rourke was wearing a green Tootal scarf with small white polka dots on it. The taller artist didn't notice this connection. The taller artist ordered the drinks. The smaller artist always drank Breton cider; the taller always a glass of vintage champagne. Lee Rourke would watch them, not because they were artists, but because they would start to argue. This they did almost dutifully, and with aplomb. The smaller of the two would always start the argument or the "verbal disagreements" as he liked to call them, with a pompous contradiction of some sort.

Lee Rourke took another longish sip from his rich, robust red. The two artists stared at each other, waiting, anticipating the spark that was about to ignite. Lee Rourke thought they looked like two dogs that had just set eyes on each other in the park: one a yapping Jack Russell and the other a graceful French Poodle.

"But that's an absurd thing to say, a spurious remark . . ."

This is how the smaller artist began the argument. He continued:

"Are you seriously trying to tell me that bendy buses are better, more aesthetically pleasing than the old Routemaster?"

"Yes . . . I am. Far more economical too . . ."

"And where does this abomination spring from?"

"They look better of course."

"They look better?"

"Yes . . . They look better. Very well designed."

"Utter rubbish! The Routemaster is a design classic!"

Their loud, self-important voices began to reverberate around the bar. Most people ignored the two artists, but Lee Rourke didn't. He ordered another fine glass of red from the rather quiet, tall, dark-haired barmaid and returned to his stool by the window. The smaller artist had jumped up in a rage and was squaring up to his taller companion. The taller artist leered down at him.

"Sit back down immediately, you drunken ape!"

"I'm not drunk."

"Yes you are . . . You're practically fried to the gills."

"I'm not."

"Listen, look at you, you're practically dribbling."

"And you're talking out of your arse!"

"And you're pissed."

"I am not pissed you pissing cunt, I was just making a stance against bad taste, this intolerable nuisance."

"What intolerable nuisance?"

"The bendy-fucking-bus!"

"This is absurd."

"You are absurd!"

The argument began to increase in volume and the smaller artist became more animated with each breath. Still no one else in the bar, apart from Lee Rourke, seemed to notice, or care for that matter. The taller artist began to shout.

"You fucking whore!"

"I beg your pardon?"

"You fucking snivelling whore! You've slept with more men than that old trout Madonna!"

"I like sleeping with men you stiff!"

"I'm NOT a stiff!"

"Yes you are . . . I've slept with you, remember? I should know!"

"Don't fucking remind me, you turdy gut! I was frigid for a fucking reason!"

"You slag!"

"YOU WHORE!"

They began to drink more and more alcohol; their shrill voices increasing in volume. Soon they could be heard out in the street. Lee Rourke noticed that still no one seemed to care: even the rather quiet, tall, dark-haired barmaid and the antipodean barman, who had now joined her, were preoccupying themselves with a particularly engrossing sudoku as if the scene unfolding just a couple of feet from them was the most natural occurrence in the world. The two artists continued:

"Your art's crap!"

"Yours is meaningless!"

"Yours is worthless!"

"Yours isn't worth the canvas it's daubed on!"

"Yours is lamentable!"

"Yours is contemptible!"

"Yours warrants nothing but my utter contempt!"

"I just said that!"

"Well, I'm saying it too!"

"You're a turd!"

"You're a shittern!"

Lee Rourke ordered yet another drink, this time he went for an expensive glass of Brouilly. He didn't mind spending what little money he had left on good French wine. Just as he took his first sip, back on his stool by the window, the smaller artist jumped up and went for the taller artist's throat.

"You stinking swine I'll have you!"

"GET OFF ME YOU BEAST!"

"You repugnant piece of rotting pig's meat!"

"PLEASE, YOU'RE STRANGLING ME! UNHAND ME!"

"You horrible decrepit slimy toad!"

"IF YOU D-D-D-DON'T . . . LET GO O-O-OF ME TH . . . THIS INSTANT I'LL BE FORCED TO HURT YOU!"

"Don't make me laugh you heartless bitch!"

"GET . . . OFF . . . ME . . . YOU . . . FUCKING . . . ZOMBIE!"

Then Lee Rourke watched as the smaller artist slugged the taller artist in the gut. The taller artist doubled over immediately, barely able to breathe. Still no one had noticed the ensuing mélêe that had now erupted. Lee Rourke momentarily looked over at the antipodean barman and rather quiet, tall, dark-haired barmaid;

they were still discussing the finer points of the joint sudoku, both hunched over their newspaper, completely oblivious. Just as Lee Rourke was about to walk over to the taller artist with the red Tootal scarf to see if he was okay something strange happened: as the taller artist eventually regained his composure he turned to the smaller artist and began to laugh uncontrollably, giving his smaller companion a manly slap on the back in the process.

"Every time you old goat . . . Every time you get me with that move . . . You've still got it, that I can assure."

"I learnt it all from Ali"

"Wondrous move . . . What do you want?"

"Same again I say!"

The taller artist, still laughing, turned to the antipodean barman.

"Breton cider and champagne, my man!"

Lee Rourke turned away. The spectacle was over. He began to

think about which bus he would take home. Maybe he should pick something up from a deli for dinner. He began to think about how all his weekends seemed to be flying by these days. He thought about that great title by Charles Bukowski: *The Days Run Away Like Wild Horses Over The Hills*. Lee Rourke had work the next day, he would wake and then leave his flat, he would walk to work, he would do this everyday until it was the weekend again. And again, the following Sunday, you would probably find Lee Rourke sitting in The French House at 3.00pm drinking fine red or white, waiting for the two artists to start their argument. And sure enough they would. And Lee Rourke would accept this fact, knowing deep down that things probably don't get much better than this.

The Pigeons of Kingsland Road

"This street/ this fucking street."

- Stephen Monaghan, '*The Kingsland Walk of Shame*'

It was quite an easy decision really, it wasn't that extraordinary, there wasn't that much thought put into it. It was just like Tony MacLaren had decided to walk out of work and head for home on a whim, like the flick of an unknown switch inside his head had just tripped rendering rational thought useless. He didn't tell anyone; calmly, he just got his coat and his bag and walked out of the door. It was the easiest thing in the world and he remembered thinking why hadn't he done it before? One foot just followed the other. He never looked back and he certainly didn't care.

It was a hot, sticky day and he walked his usual route home, northwards, straight up the Kingsland Road. Poems had been written about this particular Roman-London highway – he hadn't read them, but if he had done he would surely have understood the reasoning behind them. Kingsland Road, central North-East

London: a road only real Londoners have heard of it seemed. It was his favourite road in London, a thought that often amused him. Do other people have favourite roads? They must do. So why shouldn't he? Tony MacLaren walked everywhere, he rarely took the bus and he never took the tube – just too much hassle really. He was proud of this small fact, he had lived in London now for near on eight years and not once had he set foot into that despicable underground warren of filth, dust, and used air. The tube filled Tony MacLaren with dread, if there was one thing he was never going to do, in his rotten life, it was catch the tube. And anyway, the recent bombings had put a stop to that idea. For Tony MacLaren this was ample justification not to venture down those relentless escalators. It was all he needed. He hated all this "We're not scared" nonsense, Tony MacLaren was utterly shitting himself at the prospect of another bomb if he thought about it – which he tried desperately not to do. But he did, quite regularly. The Blitz was just an image, it meant nothing to him. It was just words. Just as this current government-sponsored mind game didn't mean a thing to him: how dare they tell me I'm not scared, he thought. So he walked. And he was happy to walk, so happy, in fact, he couldn't remember why he was walking home in the first place.

Kingsland Road is a strange place for those not accustomed to its over-the-top nuances. Its blatant flaws are suffocating; the entirety of its tumult an in-your-face reality for all who venture its length. Real yet always oddly askew. From its southern non-conformist roots to its northern disparate tip – a road of Roman origin, a road of transience, a trade route, a smuggler's paradise, a dissenter's lair, a horrible stinking cess-pit of everything that makes a city like London great.

And so Tony MacLaren continued to walk away, northwards, away from the city, away from the masses, away from his use within the grand scheme of things. It wasn't like Tony MacLaren was some kind of rebel either; such an existence was inconceivable to him – he wasn't even a member of a union. No, Tony MacLaren was tired; he just needed to escape, to silently walk away, without fuss and without protest.

It's not that he wanted to do anything spectacular with his newfound freedom, he just wanted to walk.

Kingsland Road, as usual, was loud and unrelentingly busy. Cars beeped their horns continuously and random gaggles of humans shouted and laughed and snarled, lone cyclists meandered through the traffic, beggars arched their tired necks to gain some kind of eye contact with the droves of potentially soft-hearted middle-class types with pockets brimming with change they didn't require. Two young women walked by speaking Swahili, then four Russian workmen, two Irish navvies, a plethora of Bengalis and many people in languages Tony MacLaren had never encountered before – and probably never would again. So Tony MacLaren walked home, entombed in this ever-expanding cacophony of progress.

And he found this rather odd, why do we spend all our days cooked up in some meaningless place of industry with other human beings we would rather have not met anyway when we could be out here, mixing with true progress and life? Tony MacLaren knew he would never be able to answer this question, but it didn't stop him from asking. He had often seen people walking through the city streets, encapsulated within a world of their own misunderstanding. A world generated and amplified by modernity, two little plugs in the ears – an island created in magazines and company boardrooms. Why do this? Surely, and he had realised this a long time ago, the greatest symphony is already out there? iPods are already superfluous, we don't need them anymore, and we never really have. Everything we need to listen to already exists. It was thoughts such as these that made Tony MacLaren happy.

It wasn't long before the bus hit the car – a bendy 149 hitting a rusting Peugeot 205. Side on, to be precise. At first Tony MacLaren thought it was a bomb exploding on the back seat of the bus, as did everyone else within the immediate vicinity – the images of the recent attacks still evident, still etched in the mind like a nine-inch nail embedded in a wall. The car span across the width of Kingsland Road, before shuddering to a sudden halt. It wasn't a near-miss as such, but it was a bit too close for Tony MacLaren. He found the whole scene quite ridiculous. The driver of the Peugeot looked quite dazed for a moment but, rather surprisingly, soon came around. The driver of the Peugeot looked up through his windscreen at Tony MacLaren and then back, behind him, to the bendy 149 that had screeched to an awkward halt in the middle of the Kingsland Road, its passengers shouting at its driver to continue his/their journey as if this sort of thing happened all the time – which, of course, it invariably does. The myriad impatient car owners behind beeping their horns incredulous that such a thing could happen on their particular way from A to B. Progress momentarily halted. Breakdown and confused annoyance. The driver of the 149 bus opened the door to his cab. This always looked odd wherever it happened as if bus drivers were supposed to stay in their cabs at all costs. The 149 bus driver walked over to the Peugeot 205 by Tony MacLaren. Its driver showed no emotion whatsoever. Tony MacLaren immediately thought about the driver of that bus in Tavistock Square, who just calmly stepped out of his cab and walked, deaf from the shock of the blast, west out from Bloomsbury and its jammed, chaotic environs until he was eventually picked up somewhere west of Acton.

The driver of the Peugeot 2005 opened his door, his dazed confusion quickly turning into a deep, heartfelt rage. The driver of the 149 bus held out his arms like a petulant centre-forward confronting the referee. Tony MacLaren took a step back, waiting for the imminent fireworks – he'd seen this scenario too many times before on the Kingsland Road. Most ended in a shouting match, the usual Germanic expletives hurled at each other for all they are worth for a short while until the traffic, that relentless tumult, urges them to part and get on with the formalities. Very rarely do such scenarios erupt into violence, but when they do it is often nefarious.

Tony MacLaren has seen it all on Kingsland Road: car drivers attacking bus drivers, bus drivers attacking car drivers, car drivers literally attacking buses, bus drivers literally attacking cars, pedestrians and passengers looking on, some aghast, most irritated at the hold-up in their day-to-day business, all irate, except the pigeons who just seemed to go about their daily business regardless of noise and obfuscation, and Tony MacLaren knew, he knew all too well it was the work that led to all this continued human confrontation and hostility. If there was a way for him to just walk away from it all he would, this day's little adventure was the start of something big, a change of lifestyle, maybe an escape for good, not just another weary afternoon away from his desk. Surely, all it took was a moment like this?

Tony MacLaren thought this idea over while watching the driver of the Peugeot 2005 walk casually over to the driver of the 149 bus and punch him full on the nose without even uttering one word, delivered with the stealth and precision of a man who had done such a thing numerous times before. The sound of knuckle crunching cartilage startled all within earshot. The driver of the 149 bus, a short, stocky individual, fell down to one knee. On better days he would have fought back, but there was something hanging over him. He looked up at the driver of the Peugeot 2005.

"What did you do that for?"

"You weren't looking where you were going, you could have killed me . . ."

"But I didn't see you . . ."

"You nearly put an end to it . . ."

"Please . . . I'm sorry . . . This is a difficult time for me . . . We are all, we . . . We . . . We're nervous . . . There's bombs . . ."

"We all have to do our jobs, driver . . . We all have to get on with whatever it is we do . . . That's why we work . . . We all have fucking jobs to get on with . . ."

The conversation took its usual route, as it did in most cases. Tony MacLaren walked home. Leaving the blood to pour and the trundle of everyday life to pick itself up off the floor and continue its chores. He wanted to be like a pigeon. He wanted to find the whole scenario uninteresting, he didn't want it to bother him anymore. But it did. He just wanted to get on with his life, to do his own thing, not to bother with these fidgety humans who got under his feet everyday, with their arguments, their orders, their squabbles and idiosyncrasies – their relentless myopic tumult. Tony MacLaren just wanted to get away from them and their jobs, their fashions – so he walked, he walked up the Kingsland Road and just for that fleeting moment, whilst walking away, he felt like a pigeon going about its business, oblivious to everything. It was truly wonderful. But he knew, he knew all right, he knew deep down that it couldn't last. It never did. And he knew most people felt the same.

Tony MacLaren was momentarily free. He was momentarily

beside himself, looking on, walking. Alone. Well, until the next day that is, when he would casually walk back down the Kingsland Road with tired, sleepy eyes and a hung, drawn and quartered face into work, that horrible recurring nightmare, complaining of an upset stomach, a trivial human nuisance, like everyone else did when they had temporarily had enough, when they had simply woken up and thought 'forget it'. And Tony MacLaren would hate himself for it, like he did every other day.

The pigeons would always have one over a man like Tony MacLaren. And deep down he knew that much too.

Cruel Work

It was exactly one year to the day that Lewis Dowling's then partner, Kara, finally succumb to the incurable cancer that had eaten her inside out, little by little, for the previous two years. But Kara was far from his mind on this bright, sunny evening. Lewis Dowling was thinking about the black tights the young woman was wearing in front of him as he made his way down to Aldwych to catch his bus back to Stoke Newington. Lewis Dowling had been drinking in Soho for most of the day; he had worked up a hunger.

He was thinking about how she would look underneath her clothes; wearing nothing but those black tights. She wasn't particularly attractive, her hips were too wide for his taste and she limped a little, which he found rather odd but appealing all the same. But those black tights she was wearing, those wonderful delicate fibres caressing her soft skin underneath, especially around her arse, hugging her calves and thighs – he wanted her.

Kara, who would often dress up for him in expensive lingerie herself, once told him that the sole reason men liked to penetrate women wearing tights was because somewhere – deep down – they wanted to, or imagined they were breaking-in a virgin for the very first time. Kara told him that although it was an obvious power-trip, underneath the masculine posturing, grunting and licentious braggadocio the man committing this particular pleasure was returning to something primordial and base, something, in fact, beyond pleasure. Something that he didn't understand, a common theme that had been repeated over and over throughout our evolution. Kara had enjoyed the subtle complexities of sex more than anything else.

He didn't realise this but it could be said that by watching this woman in the black tights he was, somewhere deep within, linking back to those intimate moments with Kara, and subconsciously he did, in fact, miss her: each of those numerous times she allowed him to tear slight holes in the sylphlike material clinging around her arse and crotch just waiting for him to poke his searching fingers through; the first little droplets of desire before the rampant, bestial ripping asunder, as he guided his prick inside her. Or maybe he had finally moved on, and he wanted to transfer all he'd learnt with Kara on those long nights together before she became ill. Either way he was still looking at the black tights glistening in the late sun on the woman just up ahead from him.

He had to follow her, there was no other option. He wanted to know where she was going. He wanted to speak to her, and he wanted to get his hands on her, to hear the faint cleave of fabric. She stopped suddenly to look in the window of a restaurant and then continued on her way. He altered his pace accordingly. She stopped for traffic, even bending down to look in her bag, the round curvature of her arse-cheeks near bursting through the expensive tailoring of her black pencil skirt, and all the while he hung back, casually, like it was the most natural thing in the world, watching those black tights grip her incredible form. He imagined slowly peeling the black tights down, halfway across her plump arse, kissing each cheek, caressing the silky texture between her legs, the pale skin underneath getting hotter and hotter. He imagined the conversation they would have:

"I've noticed for some considerable time now that you've been following me, why have you been following me?"

"I like what you're wearing . . ."

"Do you now?"

"Yes, very much so . . . Especially your tights . . ."

"My tights?"

"Yes, your tights . . ."

"They're just normal black silk tights . . ."

"That's exactly what I like about them . . ."

"Is it now?"

"Yes, it is . . ."

"Well maybe you'd like to join me?"

"Maybe I would . . . Where are we walking to?"

"My flat of course . . ."

He watched her tail-end wobble with each step, the repetitive sway from left to right, gravity forcing each hunk of flesh downwards, generating each ripple of pleasure within him like a stone being dropped into a clear lake. He was quite amazed really, the walk down to Aldwych was a busy one and not one other person had noticed her. He was alone; consumed by his lust.

He once followed Kara along the street without her knowing. It was in the first few weeks of their burgeoning relationship, he had seen her walking along Wardour Street in Soho. She was wearing beige figure-hugging trousers and a black jacket that complimented her average-sized frame. Rather than run up to her, he decided to follow her. She walked with a purpose, stopping only for a coffee and some cake in Bar Italia. She never once looked up from what she was doing, the task ahead – whatever that was – to observe those around her, atomised in a world of her own volition and thinking only of coffee and cake. In that moment she seemed untouchable. He liked this. He left her as she stepped on to a No 38. He saw her that very evening, as arranged. They spent the night together in his old flat on the Essex Road – this was before he'd confessed his feelings of love for her. Kara never found out about him following her that afternoon in Soho, he never thought the need to tell her. He wanted to keep that image of her to himself.

The woman wearing the black tights began to slow down, anticipating the lights near the Sicilian Arcade in Holborn. Lewis Dowling hung back, keeping one eye on the road and the other on the black tights gently embracing the back of her legs.

He imagined what he would do to her once he was inside her flat (he would do exactly what he used to do with Kara): first he would look around her bedroom, observing the things she had filled it with. He would instinctively want to know where her underwear draw was situated; once this was noted he would look through it as soon as she left the room. He would rub the silky fabric through his fingers. When she returned he would make polite chit-chat, inching closer to her all the time, then he would calmly ask her to lie on the bed. He would gently straddle her and slowly unclip her skirt, he would pull it gently down her legs and drop it onto the floor by the side of the bed. Then he would stare at her legs, her thighs, the backs of her knees, her calves, her feet, her arse cloaked in the thin, silky, teasingly transparent material of the black tights. He would slowly caress her thighs, squeezing; he would slap her arse cheeks playfully, delighting in the faint wobble of flesh, he would do this a number of times until the skin began to redden a little. He would tease the fabric near her crotch, testing its strength and durability. Then he would tear a hole, a tiny little hole, the sound of it would send shivers through him, a little sign of the paroxysms to come. He would poke a couple of his fingers into the hole, he would begin to prise it open, further, wider; she would not make a sound. She would stick out her arse, wiggle it, and then . . . he would tear the tights open in a frenzy, whilst undoing his jeans, frantically, desperately ripping the black tights asunder. He would begin to pull her knickers aside, yanking them violently. His prick would be hard and he would bask in the electrifying friction caused each time it touched the shredded fabric. He would force it up her. He would pump furiously. And then it would be over.

The traffic was busy. The pavement was busy too. Everywhere was busy. He walked down to the corner of Tavistock Street and Wellington Street. There didn't seem to be a break in the traffic, it trundled along in both directions. Cyclists weaved and wended in and out of lines of black cabs and cars and white vans, while the multitudes on foot waited patiently, and impatiently, for gaps in the traffic, to finally cross the road towards Exeter Street, Aldwych, The Strand, Savoy Street, south towards the river. This they did from every conceivable angle.

He had caught her up now and was standing beside her, waiting for a rare break in the choking traffic. He could smell her faint perfume, he inched closer to her, slowly, and the little finger of his right hand touched, gently brushed, hers. Skin touching skin. She didn't notice, it was that brisk. Electricity shot through him.

He couldn't speak to her though, not yet, not by the side of the road, near the gutter and the cars, the fumes. So he waited beside her for a gap to appear in the traffic. It seemed to take an age. Her scent began to engulf him, surround him, linger around his neck, his lips, under his nostrils – he began to shiver quite uncontrollably. He thought she could see him, sense his fear – but she couldn't, of course.

Kara had once told him that she liked the way his cheeks reddened when he was nervous; she liked the rather boyish aspect of this. She once asked him about any peculiarities he liked about her. It took him a while but he eventually told her that it was her patience he loved; nothing more and nothing less. He couldn't remember exactly what she said, something about being certain there was nothing idiosyncratic about patience.

But he did remember one thing if ever pushed: we all have to wait at some point in our lives, she would say, just some have to wait longer than others.

Suddenly a gap appeared in the traffic and she darted out into the centre of the road. Lewis Dowling had missed his chance and as soon as another gap appeared he would dash out to the centre of the road too, just like she had done. It was then that he would speak to her. Cars, fumes, it was too late to worry about that. Of course, he didn't quite know what he would say (probably something obvious about the traffic), but at least it was a start. He didn't have to wait that long for another gap it turned out . . . and then ***Blackness***. Nothing. Not even the distant flicker of a memory, like people used to say happened. Not even a faint image of Kara. Nothing.

For those around him, of course, including the woman wearing the black tights, it was the sight of the Ford Transit van hitting him full on that occupied their collective thoughts. They watched as his limp body was flung mercilessly into the air. The white Ford Transit van screeching to a halt. They watched as his head hit the bitumen with a damp thud, splitting like an egg shell, brain and blood and tooth splattering the van like Cherry Blossom falling from a tree, chunks of cranium scattered across the double yellow lines, his left foot, bereft of its shoe somehow, sock hanging half off, twitching. Of course there were the ubiquitous screams that accompany such dreadful moments, the momentary pandemonium, the disbelief, but there was also an eerie calm in the air, a feeling that everything had stopped, like a clock on a wall or a wrist noticed by its owner for the very first time – that extraordinary age before it is fixed again.

Forty-seven people attended Lewis Dowling's funeral. Old friends mostly. Most were thinking about Kara, wondering if she was present, watching over his coffin, safe. Even the atheists amongst the assembled mourners fleetingly entertained this peculiar thought before joining the rest to think about their own mortality, their own funerals. Who would be there? What would people say? Who would cry first? How would they react? The usual vainglorious, and all too human, thoughts that enter the mind at such events. Most, if asked, would agree that Kara would be quite distraught if she was alive and sitting amongst them, dressed in a Whistles black jacket and trousers, a white handkerchief in her hand, dabbing her eyes as she is consoled by her mother. Most thought it quite sad that she wasn't alive to be at his funeral.

None, as it were, gave Lewis Dowling a second thought really, as his coffin rolled into the flames. Not even on the most important day of his life. They were far too busy living their own lives; some had to get back to work, others had to sign on, pick up children from school, some were even beginning to wonder who would be staying on for drinks at the buffet provided at his favourite pub in Hackney after the flames had turned his bulk into ashes. All had other things on their minds.

Lee Rourke.

The Talbot, Hackney, East London,

January – September 2006.

Where each of these fragments were written.

(Footnotes)

[1] Like most public houses on Hoxton Market this particular one has finally succumb to the encroaching gentrification that has crept into the area. The Bacchus (now simply called 'Bacchus') is an expensive restaurant specialising in 'slow cooked' food. It is obvious to all that Charlie Bruen will never eat there.

[2] Since these sad events took place the No 38 has, indeed, bowed down to urban progress and is now, itself, one of the ubiquitous "bendybuses" to snake its way throughout London's myriad streets.